VEILED DESTINY

A gripping tale of suspicion, fear and blood vengeance...

Followed by a menacing driver down the lonely twisting lanes of the Chiltern Hills one night, Sophie Stone uses her local knowledge to evade her pursuer, and is grateful for the timely intervention of handsome Luke Despard. When a sequence of threatening events follows, Sophie begins to suspect someone wishes to kill her. Yet the only people who would benefit from her death are her business partner, Pru Bailey and Sophie's own half-brothers and sisters. After a sudden violent death, Sophie turns to Luke, but when she almost dies Sophie knows she is on her own and dare not trust anyone...

All situations in this publication are fictitious and any resemblance to living persons is purely coincidental.

VEILED DESTINY

by
Marina Oliver

Magna Large Print Books
Long Preston, North Yorkshire,
England.

British Library Cataloguing in Publication Data.

Oliver, Marina
  Veiled destiny.

  A catalogue record for this book is
  available from the British Library

  ISBN 0-7505-1252-0

First published in Great Britain by Severn House Publishing Ltd., 1997

Copyright © 1997 by Marina Oliver

Cover photography © Last Resort Photography Library

The moral right of the author has been asserted

Published in Large Print 1998 by arrangement with Severn House Publishers Ltd.

Magna Large Print is an imprint of
Library Magna Books Ltd.
Printed and bound in Great Britain by
T.J. International Ltd., Cornwall, PL28 8RW.

Chapter One

Sophie glanced in the rearview mirror and frowned. What the blazes was the idiot behind her playing at, flashing his headlights so impatiently? The lane was narrow and twisty, there wasn't room for him to overtake even if she stopped completely.

The other driver evidently realised this, for he dropped back and the headlights receded. Sophie yawned. It had been an exhausting two days, but apart from the irritation of selfish drivers, she was glad she'd decided to come home tonight instead of leaving it until morning. Then, instead of fighting against the rush hour traffic, she'd be cantering up through the beech woods on Smoke, her new mare.

Lost in dreams of the pleasures of this, steering round the familiar bends on autopilot, she didn't realise until the glare of headlights almost blinded her that the car had caught up with her again.

She narrowed her eyes and flicked the

mirror up to minimise the glare. The fool was far too close! Was he drunk or one of those crazy maniacs who loved terrorising lone women drivers?

There was a field entrance a short way ahead. Sophie flashed her indicator lights, slowed, and drew up into the gap. Let him get by, she thought angrily. I'd rather be behind such a dangerous clown.

But instead of passing her, with the derisive toot on the horn she expected, the car behind stopped too. The brakes squealed as the driver slewed to a halt almost on a level with her, blocking the road and hemming her in.

Sophie watched, momentarily incapable of action, as the driver opened his door. Well, if he meant to be rude about women drivers he'd get as good back! Road hog! He leapt out and began to run towards her. He carried something and Sophie's eyes widened in disbelief. It looked like a machete! She came back to life, jerked into first gear and bumped her car hurriedly out over the rough verge, thanking her stars it was both low and free of ditches and other obstacles. She had no desire to argue with an axe-wielding madman. As she gained the crown of the road she elbowed down the lock on the door and wound up the window which she'd opened to savour the moist fresh air of the countryside after the fumes and heat of London.

In the mirror she saw the man race back and set off after her before his car door was properly closed. By now Sophie was afraid as well as angry. But she knew all these lanes, she consoled herself. She knew every bend, every hill, every turning. Surely she could outrun that freak.

For three miles she managed to stay clear. Her local knowledge enabled her to brake at the last possible moment before a bend, take side turnings at speed, and shoot across junctions without stopping. But the driver behind took full advantage of having her as guide, and cut corners on the bends while matching her braking and accelerating only split seconds later.

Then there was a stretch of straight, narrow road, sunk deep between high banks and overhung with trees. It was barely half a mile, but the only place where overtaking was possible. If he got in front and stopped her she was lost. There would be no chance of turning the car to try and escape the way she'd come.

The big car pulled out and grimly, teeth

gritted, Sophie held to the middle of the road. To her horror she saw her pursuer draw closer. With no space to overtake it seemed as though he meant to ram into her. He was barely a couple of yards behind when Sophie, her nerve failing, swung over to her left.

With a burst of speed the big car swept past, and only the fact that Sophie had slowed down as she swerved saved her. The big car's rear end almost swiped her Fiat as it crowded past with only inches to spare, then veered straight into her path.

It was a big Volvo estate, she saw. Her Uno was no possible match for such a car, built to withstand impacts which would smash most other cars to tangled heaps of metal.

The impetus of the Volvo's speed carried it round the next corner and Sophie, already slowing down, slammed on her brakes. There was a faint chance yet of evading him. Just before the corner was a narrow side road. It led into a maze of lanes and unmade tracks which wound through the woods.

If she could gain just a quarter of a mile lead while he was turning in order to follow her, she could surely lose him.

Luckily it was full moon, light enough for her to find her way with her lights cut, and hide in one of the woodland tracks used for logging machinery. If he found her she would be able to run for it. She'd back herself against any drunken stranger to hide successfully amongst the bracken and tangled undergrowth.

Sophie went for a quarter of a mile before she came to the track she remembered. She swung off the road into a wide space, rutted from the logging machinery, and headed for the narrow track which twisted away through the trees. Then she swore under her breath. A huge tree trunk had been pulled across the path to prevent cars from using it, and there was no chance of getting past or round it. She'd have to hide here, where there was too little undergrowth.

She dived out of the car and started to run along the track, then plunged towards a solitary oak amongst the beeches. There were branches low down, and Sophie managed to swing herself up and scramble into the higher branches, finding a reasonably straight one on which she could lie, concealed. Now she had to hope that the Volvo, if it had followed her down this road, would go straight past without noticing the Fiat.

Her hopes sank as the big car drew up behind hers. The driver got out warily, peering round into the gloom and shadows out of range of the headlights which were highlighting the track. Then he moved slowly towards the track, keeping out of the light. Sophie, her eyes acclimatised to the moonlight, was watching him through gaps in the dense foliage but couldn't distinguish his features, which seemed blurred. She could see that he carried something in one hand, and was holding the other hand to his waist, as though to steady something there. If he spent long enough, or went far enough into the wood, she might be able to sneak out and get past him. Then her heart sank. He'd parked so close behind the Fiat she'd never be able to manoeuvre out before the noise of her engine alerted him.

As Sophie was resigning herself to spending a long time in the tree, until he got tired and left, she heard the sound of wheels swishing against the road, and another car, also a big one though she couldn't see what make, swung in behind

10

the Volvo, coasting down the slope without lights or engine. Sophie gulped. Was this another attacker? Why? Why was she being victimised, terrorised like this?

Sophie watched, tense, as a man stepped out of the car. He walked swiftly and silently forwards, then spoke.

'Good evening,' he said softly.

Her attacker turned with a startled oath, and Sophie jumped as there was a small flash, followed swiftly by another.

'Thank you,' the stranger said conversationally. 'That should give me some excellent shots. It's a very reliable camera. Pity your mug's covered up. But perhaps you can be persuaded to pose without that face covering.'

The fight which ensued was brief but inconclusive. The newcomer wielded what Sophie thought was a torch effectively, and knocked the machete out of the attacker's hands. As he staggered back, clutching a damaged shoulder, her rescuer tore off the stocking mask. He revealed a swarthy, black-eyed youth who snarled furiously.

'Damn you! Why did you have to interfere?' he yelled, and kicked out viciously. As the other man sidestepped to avoid the wicked metal-tipped boots, the youth ran for his car. 'I'll be back,' he shouted as he slid behind the wheel of the Volvo. 'We'll get you in the end!'

He reversed hastily out of the turning, scraped the other car, and raced back the way he'd come.

'He's scratched your car!' Sophie exclaimed indignantly. She'd spoken without thinking and then held her breath. Who was this other man? Could she trust anyone in so isolated a spot, long after midnight?

Her rescuer turned swiftly, switching on his torch and swinging the beam round, searching for her.

'It's only a scratch. He'd have done more than that to yours. But you're safe now, he's gone. You can come out of hiding. Do you know him?' There was a pause. Sophie was considering what to do. He spoke again. 'Don't worry, if we were really working together he'd not have damaged my car. But if you prefer I'll drive off.'

That decided her. 'No! Please stay! He had a machete, and he might be waiting for me again!' she exclaimed. Hastily she swung herself off the branch and dangled, horribly conscious that she was only barely decent with the brief flowery shorts and a rumpled tee shirt she'd donned in order to drive home in the hot, sultry weather.

'Do you have to shine that torch in my eyes?' Sophie asked fretfully as she hung suspended from the branch. The old oak was in full, abundant leaf, and she felt half-stifled by it, spitting leaves out of her mouth. She was ruffled, aware that her descent from the tree was undignified.

'Sorry. I was startled, didn't realise you'd gone aloft,' he apologised, and moved forward as she released the branch and dropped to the ground.

Seconds later Sophie was struggling furiously as he clasped her in his arms, and then he lost his balance and they crashed to the ground, arms and legs entangled.

'Let me go!' she panted, and to her fury heard him chuckling.

'I'm sorry,' he said again. 'I was only trying to help, it seemed a long drop, but I wasn't expecting to be bowled over by such an attractive acorn.'

They struggled to their feet and he brushed dead leaves from his immaculate grey suit. 'Shall we get properly introduced? I'm Luke Despard.'

Sophie peered at him and breathed

deeply. 'Sorry myself, I'm being silly. I'm so nervous, I panicked again. I'm Sophie Stone. I didn't know they'd put that damned trunk there, I thought I could get the car up the track and amongst the trees before he caught me up!' she added angrily.

'Did you know him? Why he was chasing you?'

'I don't know him. I saw his face briefly as he ran for the car. As far as I know I've never seen him before.'

'I thought he was trying to kill you, the way he tried to run you off the road.'

'How long were you behind us?'

'You shot across a junction and I had to slam on the brakes. At first I thought it was kids being stupid. I realised a second later that I'd seen your face in the headlights, and you looked terrified. I decided to follow.'

'It's as well for me you did. I thought I'd got away when I managed to turn down here.'

'He backed round the bend and was only a minute behind you. By then I'd cut my lights and I followed.'

'Just some drunken fool trying to show off, I suppose.'

'He didn't smell of drink, though some other smells were too painfully obvious,' Luke said slowly. 'He threatened to be back. Nor would a casual drunk be wearing this.'

He stooped to pick up the mask he'd torn from the other man's face, and Sophie, realising what it was, let out a long breath.

'I thought his face looked odd, sort of squashed, when he stopped before and got out of the car.'

'Before?' Luke demanded. 'How long had he been chasing you?' Then as she began to shiver he shook his head. 'Don't bother. How far have you to go?'

'About three miles. I was almost home.'

'Shall I follow you? Or would you prefer me to drive you and you can collect the Fiat tomorrow?'

'I'll be OK, thanks. But I would be grateful for an escort, just in case he's waiting for me. We can go round the other way, we needn't go back to the main road, the way he went.'

'Just a minute.' Luke stretched out a hand and Sophie, though wary, remained still as he touched her hair. 'A displaced spider,' he said, grinning, and she gave

15

him a doubtful look before turning away, inefficiently brushing a few leaves from her clothes.

She was shivering, and as she made to get into her car Luke spotted a sweater lying on the back seat. 'Put this on,' he ordered, 'and then I'll help you reverse out of the track.'

She waited until he'd backed out, then led him through a bewildering muddle of lanes, eventually turning in through a wide gateway. Sophie felt the familiar glow of pride as she passed the board with the name 'Crispins', and in smaller letters below, 'Riding Stables and Livery'. They stopped on the wide tarmacked drive behind a Mini and a Ford Escort. The house was long and low, and several windows were still lit despite the lateness of the hour.

'I haven't thanked you properly,' Sophie said as she clambered from the Fiat and came across to him. 'I've delayed you and taken you out of your way, but I'm so very glad you were there.'

'Sophie, is that you?'

The door of the house opened and light spilled out across the drive. A woman appeared in the doorway.

'Pru? Why are you still up? I told you not to wait up for me.'

'Guy's still here. Who's this? Are you OK?'

'It's a long story, and I'm dying for a drink. Will you come in and have one?' she added turning to Luke.

Luke locked his Audi and followed them into a huge old kitchen, where a large pine table stood in the centre with half a dozen chairs about it. An intense-looking man in his late twenties sat at one of them, a mug and used plate in front of him. Two old and comfortable looking armchairs were either side of a big Aga, behind them doors to other rooms. One wall was dominated by an enormous old pine dresser. Instead of cooking pots and crockery, however, the shelves were filled with books and files and silver cups, while coloured rosettes were pinned on every available edge. On the opposite, window side was a modern, functional row of kitchen units and equipment, and behind the door from the hall were a four-drawer filing cabinet and a big desk holding a computer and printer.

Pru, tall and blonde, had taken one look at Sophie's white face and poured a couple of inches of whisky into a tumbler.

'Drink this,' she said firmly. 'What would you like, Mr—sorry, I don't know your name?'

'Luke Despard. I'll have whisky too, please.'

Sophie had dropped into another of the chairs by the table, nodded and smiled briefly at the man there, and waved to Luke to join her.

'This is Prudence Bailey, my partner.' She turned to the other man. 'We haven't met, but I assume you're Guy Harrington? Hi there.'

'Hello, Sophie. I've heard a lot about you from Pru.'

Pru sat beside her, the bottle conveniently nearby. 'What is this?'

'Some madman tried to kill me, and Luke drove him off,' Sophie explained tersely. 'At least, that's what it looks like, though I find it hard to believe. I think I've been dreaming.'

Luke explained, seeing that Sophie was fighting to retain her composure. By the time he'd finished, the whisky had calmed her and she was able to add details of the chase before he'd come on the scene.

'I thought he was just some drunk, but

he was wearing a mask.' She dragged the bedraggled and torn stocking from her bag, where she'd stuffed it as she got back into the car. 'It had to be deliberate. I suppose it was someone out for kicks, lying in wait for a woman on her own.'

Pru was on her feet and reaching for the wall phone.

'I'll ring the police. Did you get the number of the car?'

Sophie shook her head. 'I was too busy trying to get out of his way. It was a Volvo estate, though, black or dark blue, I think.'

'I'll have the number when my film is developed,' Luke said quietly. 'I took a couple of snaps, and one of him, though with the mask it will be impossible to identify him from that.'

'You calmly took photos? So that explains the flashes of light! I'd been puzzling over them,' Sophie said.

'It's second nature, I always have a small automatic camera in my pocket. I'm a photo-journalist, you see,' Luke explained, showing his camera to them. 'I suppose the quickest way of developing it would be to give the film to the police.'

Pru had been dialling, and speaking quietly into the phone.

'They'll be here in half an hour. Shall we have some coffee? And is either of you hungry?'

'I didn't have a meal, I thought I'd eat when I got home. I'm ravenous!' Sophie discovered.

'I could use a sandwich or some biscuits, it's hours since I had dinner.'

Guy stood up. 'Look, if you'll excuse me, I'll be on my way. You can manage without me, and I have a plane to catch first thing. Hope the police catch him. Bye, everyone.'

Pru went to see him out, while Sophie assembled bread and butter and cheese. When Pru returned she briskly ordered Sophie to sit down. Sophie grinned at her. 'It's getting serious with Guy? You've only known him for six months, and he's been abroad most of that time.'

Pru flushed. 'I told you he'd arrived here when I phoned you yesterday. You don't mind him staying, I imagine? If you got a man of your own you might be less interested in my affairs!' She shook her head as if to clear it. 'Sorry, love, I'm edgy, but I hate the idea of not seeing

20

him again for months while he's in some dreadful desert.'

They were eating the last of a pile of thick cheese sandwiches when the police arrived. Sophie told them what had happened, and Luke what he'd seen.

'The car number plate will be on the film,' he said as he handed over the camera. 'When can I have the rest of the prints back? I need some of them for an article I'm working on.'

'You'll be able to pick them up tomorrow—that is, this afternoon, I expect, sir. Where are you staying?'

'I'm on my way to Oxford. Can you phone me at the Randolph?'

'You can't go there tonight,' Sophie said quickly. 'It's way past three o'clock now.'

'The Randolph will have night porters,' Pru said but Sophie shook her head determinedly.

'No, it's another forty minutes to drive.' She turned to Luke. 'You can have the spare room here, if you like.'

'Thanks, I'd be grateful. I doubt I'd ever find my way out of this maze in the dark.'

'Sophie, you look dead beat, get to bed. I'll show Luke the spare room. You have a bag in the car?'

Pru organised them, and ten minutes later Sophie was oblivious while Luke, lying in bed in the next room, watched the dawn as he went over the details of the last few hours with considerable satisfaction.

★ ★ ★ ★

Sophie woke to the clattering of pails and looked blearily at her watch. Nine o'clock, and she was still in bed! As she pushed back the duvet recollection of the previous night's terrifying chase flooded back, and she shivered. What would have happened to her if Luke had not been there and taken a hand? She was certain she wouldn't have been found in her tree, but then she'd been certain he couldn't have followed her once she'd turned out her lights. Only the misfortune of the tree trunk blocking the track had foiled her first attempt at escape. Who knows what other accident or piece of ill-luck might have betrayed her?

Thrusting aside the thoughts of it she padded to the bathroom. After a shower she'd be able to cope. She glanced at the door of the spare room as she passed. Was Luke Despard really there? Was he as handsome as she recalled? Just under six feet, she estimated, slim built but with a muscular frame, and five or six years older than she was. His hair was a bright blond, long and streaked by the sun, and his deep tan also indicated long hours outdoors somewhere hotter than England. She wondered where.

Shaking herself impatiently at her wandering thoughts, Sophie stepped under the shower and gasped as the spray drenched her. She still had leaves in her hair, and she shampooed it, thankful for the straight simple style that dried and fell into the usual smooth cap so easily. Then she soaped herself, turned the control to cold, and stoically waited for a rapid count of ten while the cold water rinsed her, then stepped out to rub some warmth into her body as she towelled herself dry. Ten minutes later, in jeans and a tee shirt, she went into the kitchen.

'Good morning.'

Luke was sitting at the table, nursing a huge mug of black coffee. Pru was frying bacon which sizzled in the pan.

'Did you sleep OK?' she asked.

'Too well,' Sophie said ruefully. 'I meant to take Smoke out this morning, now there won't be time. I hope you were

OK, Luke? Did the noise outside wake you?'

'That's OK, I ought to get moving soon anyway. I gather you have a riding school out there?'

'Joanna and Beth have everything under control, Sophie. You can ride later. Sit down and have some breakfast,' Pru said calmly.

'Just coffee and toast for me. Yes,' Sophie replied as she helped herself to coffee. 'It's a livery stable too, we have a dozen horses of our own, the same at livery. What kind of journalism do you do?'

'A mixture of travel pieces and celebrity interviews. At the moment I'm interviewing retired politicians for a series. I saw one at St Albans yesterday, and have another lined up for tomorrow outside Oxford. I was intending to spend today looking up some old friends.'

'When will you be able to get your film back from the police? Did they say? I don't remember.'

'I'll collect it later today. Any new thoughts on why someone wants to kill you?'

'I don't believe it, I can't. If it had

been you and someone wanted to prevent some exposé article or book, it would be more believable, but I'm no threat to anyone!'

It was clearly what she wanted to believe, and Luke changed the subject. Pru set a plate heaped with bacon and eggs in front of him, and despite her protests another in front of Sophie.

'Eat it. I've had mine.'

'Where's Mrs Miller?'

'She wanted the day off to go to some WI outing. How did your London trip go? I was so taken up with the rest of it I didn't ask.'

'I saw the bank manager and the solicitor, signed all the documents, then showed three agents round the flat and appointed one,' Sophie said briefly. 'It all went smoothly.'

'Do you have to go up again?'

'No. Don't worry, I won't have to leave you to cope apart from a couple of days when I'll have to clear out the furniture. The agent advised me to leave it in place. Apparently people prefer seeing property that looks occupied.'

'Poor Sophie, having to deal with all that. What about her books?'

'She had quite a valuable collection, and I should be able to interest a library or a dealer. My aunt was an art historian,' she explained to Luke. 'She died a few months ago and we've just got probate.' She turned back to Pru. 'I cleared Aunt Meg's personal stuff, and brought all her private papers home with me to go through later. They're in the car, in two big boxes. I'd better get them out. I was too exhausted last night. Then if you really can manage without me, I'll take Smoke out. She'll be getting lazy.'

'And I must be going,' Luke said. 'That was a magnificent breakfast, Pru. Let me help you in with the boxes first.'

Sophie smiled her thanks, and after the boxes were deposited in the kitchen asked if he'd like to see round the stables. 'Unless you're in a hurry,' she added quickly.

'No hurry, I didn't fix any appointments, I was going to chance my friends being available, and if they weren't I'd wander round old haunts for the day.'

They went outside again and Sophie showed Luke the two rows of loose boxes, the big barn which had been converted into a covered school, and the jumping

26

paddock. Then they strolled round half a dozen small paddocks where several horses grazed on the lush summer grass. When he mentioned having ridden as a boy she impulsively suggested he might like to ride with her before he set off.

'If you'd like to, that is,' she added shyly. 'I don't mean to delay you.'

Luke looked at the clear blue sky. 'It's a wonderful day, and a ride through these woods would be better than Oxford with hordes of tourists and foreign language students milling about,' he replied. 'I'd love to, if you're not needed to work in the stables.'

'Pru says she can cope, she wasn't expecting me and won't have me down for anything like a special lesson,' Sophie said easily. 'I wasn't due to come back until today, but I finished early and couldn't bear another night in a dreary London flat. Are those jeans OK?'

'They'll be fine, if you can lend me a hat.'

Sophie nodded. 'Those shoes will do. You aren't a beginner, are you?'

'I rode to hounds for a couple of years,' Luke reassured her. 'I can manage most hacks.'

'Good. I didn't want to put you on a horse you can't manage, but Samson could do with an outing. He was my grandfather's horse, and he's old, but still lively, and we can't put children on him, so he isn't used a great deal. I keep him out of sentiment, I suppose. He doesn't earn his keep.'

Half an hour later they were riding through the beech woods. Sophie's mare, Smoke, was a spirited ride but Sophie managed her with ease, allowing her to sidle and prance while she got over her first excitement at being out of the paddock, and settling into a fast canter as soon as they reached a straight grassy ride. When Sophie reined in and Luke drew alongside she explained that her grandfather had taught her to ride.

'I used to come here for almost every holiday from school,' she said. 'I came to live here, to help him run the stables, when I left school, but he died a year later and left them to me. One day I'm going to open a sanctuary—you know, for horses too old to work, or ones that have been ill-treated.'

'And Pru?'

'I've known Pru for years. She was always

round here, mucking out in exchange for rides. She's lived in the village for ever, and I believe her family go back to the dark ages.'

'She's your partner? Or an employee?'

'Partner. The stables were actually quite run down. Grandfather was old, and didn't have much cash to spare. I wasn't sure I'd be able to run them on my own, but when Pru suggested putting in some money to refurbish them I offered her a partnership. Her husband had just died, you see, and she had the insurance. She sold her house to buy a half share.'

'Husband? She's older than you, but she must have married young.'

Sophie laughed. 'Straight from school, and he was quite a lot older. I wasn't here, but I gather it caused quite a stir. Not that Pru would care, she always did exactly what she liked and ignored the gossip. There's a lot of that in small villages. How are you feeling? Not too stiff?'

'I'll be stiff tomorrow, but at the moment I'm loving it. Why? Do you need to go back?'

Sophie shook her head. 'If you don't mind, I thought we could ride over to where that idiot tried to attack me. It's not very far across country. We might find something in daylight. Tyre tracks or something.'

Luke nodded. 'Good idea. I'd been thinking of going back there myself. The police didn't seem to take it too seriously, I doubt if they'd go themselves.'

'They thought it was just a joyrider,' Sophie said, 'but I can't quite believe they'd have been so determined! This way, we can cut through these fields if you can manage a couple of low hedges.'

It took half an hour to reach the spot where Sophie had been driven from her car the previous night. They dismounted, tied the horses to convenient trees, and began to search the ground. They found the machete almost immediately and Sophie pulled a length of twine from her pocket and tied it to her saddle.

'Too dry for the tyres to have left any marks,' Luke said after a while. 'You drove within inches of this trunk, he was a yard or so behind you, and my car was a couple of yards behind his, partly across the entrance. Aha!' He crouched down and held out a scrap of paper. 'A receipt for petrol, which must have fallen out of the side pocket when I got out of the car. Yes, it's from when I filled up yesterday just outside St Albans. I wonder if he dropped anything else?'

For twenty minutes or so they crawled round on hands and knees searching the ground minutely. At last Sophie sat back on her heels with a sigh.

'It's useless,' she said. 'In any case, what could it tell us if we found a sweet wrapping or a cigarette end?'

Luke didn't reply. He was half concealed under a tangle of bramble bushes. Then, slowly, he backed out and turned to face Sophie. 'I had a fleeting impression he'd dropped something,' he said quietly. 'It could have been this.'

He had pulled a handkerchief out of his pocket, and used it to hold the object he was showing Sophie. She rose to her feet and took a hurried step towards him.

'Be careful! Don't touch, there may be fingerprints.'

'But it's a gun!'

'Sawn off shotgun,' Luke agreed. 'And it hasn't been here for long, I'd say. We'd better get back and call the police again.'

Chapter Two

By the time the police had been again, escorted Sophie and Luke to the place where they had been found, and taken charge of the machete and shotgun, it was late afternoon.

'We've checked on the car, thanks to your photos,' Luke was told by the detective who was questioning them. 'It was reported stolen yesterday afternoon, but so far hasn't been spotted. I expect it's been dumped by now.'

'Will you keep us informed?' Luke asked. 'Here's my London address. I expect to be there for the next few weeks, but you could leave a message on the machine if I'm out, and I'll get it quickly.'

'You're very concerned,' the policeman commented. 'Yet I understand you were just a casual passer-by.'

Luke nodded. 'It was pure chance I became involved, yes, but I am involved. For all I know the maniac took my car registration and may be able to trace me.

He may hold a grudge. One thing surprises me. He must be aware he lost the gun there, so why didn't he go back as soon as it was light to try and retrieve it?'

The detective shook his head. 'All kinds of reasons. Maybe he hasn't got wheels now. He might not have been able to find the place. Some of these lanes look identical, and it's pretty confusing if you don't know the area. Or he may have to keep up a pretence at a job, for instance, and can't afford to arouse suspicion.'

Eventually he left, and Pru came in to drink the tea Sophie had made. She was edgy, complaining about the disruption to the work of the stables, and that she hadn't been able to prepare the meal she'd planned for that evening.

'We take it in turns to cook, when it's Mrs Miller's afternoon off,' Sophie explained to Luke. 'My limit's chops or shepherd's pie.'

'Then let me take you both out for a meal,' Luke suggested quickly. 'I noticed the pub in the village has a restaurant. If you don't mind going early I can get to Oxford in reasonable time.'

For a moment Sophie thought Pru was going to say no, but then she shrugged and smiled. 'Sorry, I'm rather edgy today, with all that peculiar business and having to work as well. I have another hour to do, then I'll be ready.'

She brusquely refused Luke's offer of help, but didn't demur when Sophie went out to help with the evening chores. When they had finished she grasped Sophie's arm and drew her into an empty loose box.

'Sophie, be careful.'

'What do you mean?'

'You know what I mean. Luke Despard. We know nothing about him.'

'I know that he rescued me from a madman,' Sophie retorted.

'You've never been particularly interested in men, only had a few boyfriends,' Pru went on, 'although I'm always urging you to find one.'

'Don't worry, I'm not falling for him any more than I'm falling for your brother!' Sophie said, wondering if it was really true. She'd felt an instant pull of attraction the moment she'd literally fallen into Luke's arms.

'John adores you, and he'd make a wonderful husband,' Pru said sadly.

'I know, Pru. But if I do marry I want to love my husband as well as be loved.

And I'm sorry, but I don't love him.'

'He's not like other men, after your money.'

'He's about the most unworldly man I know, I agree. But three times I've got friendly with a guy, only to discover it's not me he wants, but what I can give him. Don't worry, Pru, I'm not going to fall for any man, not even a good-looking charmer like Luke. But I do perhaps owe him my life. I thought I could hide from that idiot, but now I know he had a gun as well as a machete I'm not so sure I'd have got away by myself At the very least I'd have had an extremely uncomfortable night and a long walk, as he'd probably have wrecked the Fiat. And unless you want beans on toast, we'll accept Luke's offer of a meal!'

Pru laughed. 'OK, so long as you know what you're doing.'

'I do, and it's not falling head over heels in love with a man I've known less than twenty-four hours. You might believe it was love at first sight with your Guy but that's not for me.'

Or wasn't, she thought later as she dithered between the green dress which matched her eyes and the blue one which she wore for formal village occasions. Why

35

was she worrying? Normally she didn't give a toss which she wore so long as she was clean and tidy. But she hadn't fallen for Luke. She knew barely a thing about him. But he was successful in his career, as well as sophisticated and handsome, unlike anyone she'd ever met before.

They walked to the Grapes, a seventeenth century thatched inn in the centre of the village, which had been extended to the back a few years earlier to provide a small restaurant. In a short time it had gained a reputation for excellent and imaginative food, and at weekends diners had to book well in advance to be sure of a table. Sophie had told Luke they would have no problems mid-week, so she was a little surprised when she discovered that he'd telephoned to reserve a table.

'He was pretty confident we'd come,' Pru muttered as they found seats in the bar and Luke went to order their drinks.

'He's the careful sort,' Sophie replied. 'It would have been a letdown if the place had been full after all.'

It was another warm evening, and when they were shown to their table the first thing Sophie noticed was that several pairs of French windows to the garden had been opened. A man was just going through them, and she was tempted to ask whether they could sit outside. The tables scattered on the lawn were not laid for meals, though, so she sat at the table indicated, beside one of the open windows, and took the menu the waitress offered. The scent of lilac and jasmine drifted in, and they had an excellent view of the garden brilliant with flowers and flowering shrubs.

While Sophie was trying to decide between chicken filled with crab or the seafood platter which, she knew from her last visit, came with the most delicious sauce she'd ever tasted, another waitress halted beside them.

'I'm sorry, Miss Stone, but did you see where the man at that table went?' she asked.

Sophie glanced round. 'Hello, Josie. Which table?'

'The one in the corner.'

Sophie could see an empty soup bowl and a napkin thrown down half on top of it. 'There was no one sitting there when we came in. I expect he's gone to the loo.'

Josie frowned, cleared away the empty bowl, and went back to the kitchen. Sophie decided on the chicken, and they ordered. She forgot about the vanishing diner until Steve, the owner of the pub, came in with Josie twenty minutes later. He spoke to a few other people, then came across to greet Sophie and Pru, and be introduced to Luke.

'Luke Despard? I've read some of your interviews. And the travel articles. You always make me want to abandon all this and rush out to wherever.'

'I trust you won't. Now I've discovered this place I shall bring all my difficult interviewees here to soften them up. Are you the chef?'

'Only for the sweets and pastries. My brother does the rest. But I wondered if you'd seen the man who was sitting over there? He hasn't come back, and he's nowhere else in the building.'

'Left without paying, has he?' Pru asked.

'Luckily he only had the soup!' Steve said, grinning at her. 'I can stand that loss. I just don't like mysteries. Vanishing guests aren't good publicity. Well, I don't suppose he'll be coming back, so you may as well reset the table, Josie. Good to meet you, Mr Despard. Hope to see you again soon.'

'That's a certainty.'

Replete, they strolled back towards the stables, and Luke, refusing another coffee, collected his belongings and stowed them in the car. 'I'll telephone when I'm back in London,' he said as he prepared to get in. 'Let me know if anything else happens. Bye.'

Sophie slept fitfully. She re-lived the wild chase in the car, and shivered as she thought of what could have happened if Luke had not appeared. Part of her inability to sleep, though, was due to Luke. She'd never met anyone quite like him. Although she'd known many of her stepfather's friends, she'd been a schoolgirl then. Since working at the stables she'd met lots of the local people, especially the riding fraternity, but she'd never lost sleep over any of them. Several had asked her out, and once or twice she'd accepted, but they'd either been too eager to get her into bed or boring to talk to, their horizons limited to farming or horses. And much as she loved horses she felt that there were other things to life too. Pru's brother John, who was a social worker in Oxford, had been even less interesting, and despite

Pru's frequently expressed wish that he and Sophie might get together, Sophie knew she could never even contemplate it. John was worthy, but not in the least exciting or even physically attractive.

Besides, none of them was subtle. They mentioned, too soon, her father's fame and fortune. One early encounter, when she was only sixteen, and had almost been taken in by one of her step-father's employees who'd seemed so delightfully charming and sophisticated, had made her abnormally wary. The first hint of interest in her father and how his money had been left put an abrupt end to their hopes. Luke hadn't even mentioned him. Perhaps he didn't know, but it wasn't a great secret. Perhaps, a cautious streak within her insisted, he was just more subtle. Perhaps, a romantic part of her hoped, he hadn't connected her with her famous father. It was possible. When her parents had divorced her mother had returned to Britain and changed her name from Stein to the English version, Stone.

She turned over and tried to go to sleep. Would she see him again? She couldn't ring him. Would he ring her? Surely he'd want to know if the police discovered anything about her attacker? Would they? Her mind swung round to the chase again, and as dawn lightened the sky she eventually gave up all hope of sleeping and crept downstairs to take Smoke for an unexpectedly early ride.

★ ★ ★ ★

For three days life went on as normal, then early one morning as Sophie was riding Smoke up the track leading towards the woods, she rounded a bend and pulled the mare to a halt. Just where the track crossed a lane a man was sprawled on the verge, ominously still. Had he been hit by a car?

'Hello, there,' Sophie called, and when there was no response she swung down from the saddle, tied Smoke to a handy fence rail, and went towards him. His face was hidden, a jacket pulled up over his head, but she could see no blood. She was bending down trying to feel for a pulse when a sound behind her made her swing round in alarm. Another man, in the now familiar stocking mask, was running towards her, and as Sophie leapt to her feet and began to back away the supposed body came to life and jumped up too.

'Got you!' one of them said, and before Sophie could get back to Smoke they'd grabbed her arms and begun to drag her towards the road. She screamed, and caught a glimpse of a car hidden in a field entrance before there was a flurry of yellow fur and one of her attackers let go of her with a yelp of pain.

'Good boy, Sam!' a voice called, and then Sophie was released as a shotgun was fired close by. She stumbled, and saw the two men hurling themselves into the car as an excited dog pranced round, waiting for an opportunity to get in another nip.

The car raced away, and Sophie looked up to see an anxious face peering at her from across the fence. It belonged to a neighbour, Bob Jenkins, and he had a shotgun trained in the direction the car had gone.

'Are you OK?' he asked. 'What was happening?'

'Bob? I'm so glad to see you! I'm not sure. One of them was lying on the grass, pretending to be hurt, I think. Then they tried to drag me into the car. Thank goodness you're out early. And good Sam,' she added, bending to pat the half-grown retriever who was panting hard and eagerly trying to lick her face.

'I was after some pigeons. I'll walk back with you. It seems as though someone's got a grudge against you,' he added. 'Heel, boy!'

'Come in and have some coffee.'

Sophie handed Smoke over to Beth when they got back to Crispins, saying she'd be out soon to groom the mare. Then she took Bob to the kitchen. He wore a shabby old jacket, loose trousers, and mud-encrusted boots. 'Sit!' he roared suddenly at the dog, who sat down abruptly with a pained glance at his master and a tentative wag of his tail.

Pru was standing by the Aga in her dressing gown, looking bleary-eyed. 'Bob, Sophie, what's happened? You're looking pale. Sit down.'

Bob took one of the armchairs, Sophie poured coffee, and Pru sank into the other armchair.

'You're out early,' she said, yawning. 'You're almost as bad as Sophie, she gets up at dawn some days.'

'Fortunate for Sophie that I was,' Bob said, and explained what had happened.

'You can't put that down to a crazy

joyrider,' Pru said, all trace of sleepiness gone. 'I wonder if someone's trying to kidnap you? Hold you to ransom?'

As they stared at one another they heard the sound of a car stopping outside, a door slammed, and a moment later Luke halted at the open door.

'Hello, I'm not too early for you, I hope.'

'Luke! Come in,' Sophie said, astonished at his sudden appearance. 'Like some coffee?'

'Please. I decided to set off for home before breakfast was being served. How are you all? Have the police discovered anything fresh?'

'Police?' Bob exclaimed. 'Sophie, what is this?'

Distracted, Sophie tried to introduce them and explain all at once. 'Luke Despard, Bob Jenkins, a neighbour. Luke saved me the other night when some idiot chased my car, Bob. Now you've apparently foiled another attempt. But it's ridiculous!' she declared. 'It can't be true! Who could want to kill, or kidnap me?'

'It's not ridiculous, not after the other night,' Luke said decisively, 'Have you

44

phoned the police yet?'

'No time. I'd better dress, then make sure no one goes out alone today. They might still be waiting, and they might be trying to kidnap anyone from here,' Pru said, and swept out of the kitchen.

'They might try again?' Sophie stared, aghast. 'But that's unlikely. We're not the only riders, there are quite a few people round about who stable their own horses and who'd see them.'

Luke was by the phone, and as he talked the others waited grimly. Sophie poured more coffee, filled a bowl with water for Sam, and slumped into one of the armchairs. Pru returned and stood leaning against the sink, drinking her coffee.

'Could it be someone with a grudge against the stables?' she asked. 'Do you remember last month, when two of the livery horses got out of their stalls? Is someone trying to sabotage us?'

'That could have been an accident, the doors weren't fastened properly. We were short-handed that day, and everyone was rushed.'

'We were short-handed because that girl Tricia decamped during the night, and it was Beth's day off. She never came back, and didn't have the nerve to ask for the money we owed her. I suppose she found it was too much like hard work.'

'A new employee?' Luke asked sharply.

'Yes. Why? What can she have to do with this? She's gone now,' Sophie replied a trifle impatiently.

'How long had she been here?' he persisted quietly.

Pru looked curiously at him. 'Only a couple of weeks.'

'Where did she come from? Did you take up references? Had she a P45?'

'She'd just come here from Ireland, to get experience in an English stable, she said. She had a couple of old references from stables in County Cork, and I phoned them. They seemed OK, though she'd been abroad for a good few years, they said, as an au pair. And she was good with horses, knew what she was doing, and rode well, though she hadn't a lot of patience with the youngsters. She didn't have any teaching qualifications. And she didn't have a P45, she filled in a P44 which I've sent off already.'

'Probably with false details. Look, this gets more and more suspicious. I have to go back to London, but may I come back this evening and talk it over, when we know what the police have found?'

'Come and have a proper meal,' Sophie suggested. She smiled, but her eyes were dark with worry.

'Thanks. And don't leave the house today, Sophie.'

'I can't let the others do all the work!'

'Then make sure you're always with someone you can trust, and don't go away from the stables or the paddocks. I'd suggest no one goes off the premises until the police have checked the paths you use, either.'

'I'll stay here if you like,' Bob offered. 'Sam will warn us if anyone strange approaches.'

'He'll raise the roof if anyone comes, won't you, boy?' Pru patted the dog who was sprawled underneath the table. 'Thanks, Bob, an extra pair of eyes will be very welcome. And no doubt the police will want to talk to you as well as Sophie, and see exactly where this happened.'

Luke departed soon afterwards, passing the police car as he reached the main road which, they had assured him, would take him towards the M40 and London.

It was seven o'clock before he returned.

Hearing voices from beyond the house he walked round, past the entrance to a large stable yard, and onto a west-facing terrace behind.

The house was Georgian, built of the typical Chiltern brick and flint. He thought it must once have been a farm, as there were several large barns beyond the stables. It looked prosperous, the buildings and the ranch fenced paddocks all around in immaculate condition. Clearly a lot of money had been spent on refurbishing it. The terrace, of old York stone, was wide and ran for a greater length than the house. At the far end was a swimming pool. Sophie and Pru were relaxing on loungers, both displaying shapely bikini-clad figures.

'You're a marvellous watchdog!' Luke said disgustedly as Sam, sprawled at Sophie's feet, opened one eye and wagged a feeble tail. 'Where's Bob?'

'Gone home to change. He's coming to supper too, but he's been walking round all the bridleways today with the police, to see if they could find any traces of anything else odd. That's why Sam is knackered,' Sophie explained. 'Do you want to have a swim before we eat? There are some spare trunks somewhere.'

'No, thanks, I'll pass.'

'Have a beer, then. Or something stronger?'

'Beer's fine.'

'Was it a busy day?' Pru asked as Sophie delved into a coolbox beside her chair and produced several cans and glasses.

'Quite easy, for once. A member of the last government. He was a good subject, willing to talk, not someone I had to keep prompting all the time.'

'I'd have thought all politicians were willing to talk,' Sophie remarked.

'You'd be surprised. Some of them are so concerned about the image they present, and what history will say about them, they're even cagier than when they were in office. Thanks. Cheers.' He drank deeply. 'That's better! Now, what did the police say?'

'Not much they could say,' Pru said shortly. 'They didn't find any clues where it happened. They'll send a patrol car round occasionally, and suggested we warned all the riders we knew to be careful, not to ride alone.'

'They probably won't try this again,' Luke said slowly. 'Have any strangers been

49

seen about recently?'

'There are always strangers about, and strange cars parked. It's popular walking country,' Sophie replied. 'Oh good, here's Bob. We'll go and change while you have a beer, and supper will be ready in ten minutes.'

Luke waited until the girls had disappeared, then turned to the older man. 'You're a neighbour, I understand?'

'Yes, my house is over there, you can just see it behind the big barn. I retired there six years ago, just before Sophie came to live at Crispins with her grandfather. He started the livery stables, and left the business and the house to her when he died three years ago.'

'Is there any chance it's some local rivalry, sabotage, as Pru suggested this morning? You must know the people round here.'

Bob shook his head.

'There's business rivalry. With set aside and less need for agricultural land, a couple of the farmers round here are starting similar projects, livery and riding stables. But it's not as easy as they may have hoped. Sophie's stables have been here longest, and are well established.

Besides, there's been less money to spend on luxuries like riding of late, so less demand. But I can't believe anyone local would deliberately try to harm the girls or wreck their business. Pru's lived in the village all her life, her family was well respected, and Sophie's been coming here for holidays since she was a tot. And surely kidnapping's a bit extreme?'

'Then it's personal. Someone has a grudge against Sophie, probably unconnected with the stables.'

'And they want to hold her to ransom? How did you get involved the other night? From what they've told me that could have been an attempted kidnap too.'

Luke told Bob all the details he could, and the older man was shaking his head in disbelief when Sophie came to call them into the kitchen.

For a while, as they ate a tasty chicken casserole, followed by strawberries and cream, they talked of other things. Luke told stories about his work, and Bob responded by talking about his former job as a university librarian.

As Pru cleared away the dishes and poured coffee there was a silence. Then Sophie sighed and turned to Luke.

'Did you know the police discovered the car, the Volvo which chased me, abandoned in High Wycombe, in a car park near the motorway junction? It had been stolen the day he chased me.'

'I knew it was reported stolen at four o'clock on that day. The woman was collecting her children from a school in Hampstead, left her keys in the car, and while she was talking to the other mums it was taken. No one saw anything, of course.'

'If he abandoned it in Wycombe, perhaps he lives there?' Pru suggested.

'He could just as easily have hitched a lift to London or Birmingham, or south to the M4. Or been picked up by arrangement.'

'Luke! That means it was planned, a conspiracy!' Sophie protested.

'If it had been just the car, I could have believed it was chance he followed you. With men lying in wait near a bridleway you use frequently, plus the mysterious Tricia from Ireland, it begins to look more deliberate. She could have been sent here to spy out your routine.'

'Did you see anyone following you earlier? That day you came back from London?' Pru asked.

Sophie shook her head. 'I don't believe they're connected. If he'd killed me in the car it could have been put down to an accident. The kidnapping—well, they could have been waiting for someone else and apart from that it was so deliberate, it would be bound to make the police suspicious.'

'Did you see anyone following you in London?' Pru repeated.

'There wasn't much traffic, but there's always some in London and on the motorway. I don't remember if anything followed me.'

'I think you said you were in London sorting out an aunt's flat? How could they have known you were coming home so late?' Luke asked.

'The flat belonged to my great-aunt Meg, who died a few months ago. It's in Holland Park. I was so fed up I couldn't bear to sleep there another night, so I set off just before midnight.'

'So it's likely someone was watching you there. Did people know you were going to be in London?'

'I mentioned it to a few. I couldn't go until after the church fete, because we always give rides there.'

'They knew where your aunt lived?'

'Possibly. She was Grandfather's sister and she grew up here. And knew lots of the villagers.'

'Did Tricia know you were planning this?'

'She could have done. But Luke, why should anyone be trying to kill or kidnap me? I can't believe someone was watching me in London! It's too bizarre! The more I think about it, it must have been a joyrider if the car was stolen. Some of those idiots can get vicious, and carry guns to make them feel macho. The other was just a horrid coincidence. It's just not credible anyone would devise such elaborate plans to kidnap me, a whole gang of them, sending spies to work here weeks beforehand!'

As Bob was leaving Luke moved with him to the door.

'I've something to fetch from the car,' he explained.

As soon as they were outside he turned to the older man.

'You don't believe it was pure bad luck, do you?' he asked.

'Of course it wasn't, but no point in scaring them both to death. I'll try to keep an eye open, ask around to see if there have been any nosy strangers about, and make sure they take sensible precautions.'

'Here's my card. Will you let me know any developments? I feel involved.'

Bob nodded. 'I'll phone if I discover anything. You'd better have my number.'

Luke wrote it down. 'I shall be at my London flat for several weeks now. I'm working on a travel book as well as the interviews. Please, will you try to warn me if you hear Sophie's going anywhere on her own? I'll find an excuse to go with her if it's at all possible.'

Bob glanced at him, smiling slightly. 'Nice lass, Sophie. I'm amazed she hasn't been snatched up years ago. Too fond of her horses for much socialising, I suppose. Sam, here, boy! Goodnight, Luke, glad to have met you.'

★ ★ ★ ★

The next week passed quietly. They interviewed several girls who'd applied for the vacancy Tricia's departure had caused, and appointed a cheerful redhead, Caroline. Sophie fretted when Pru insisted she never rode out alone, for she'd enjoyed her early rides before the pressures of the day crowded in. It was only common sense, she knew, until the police had either discovered the culprits or frightened them off. She refused to believe it was an attack on herself, and even began to wonder whether she had exaggerated the menace of the car chase.

It was with a sense of relief she heard from the estate agents selling her great-aunt's flat that they had a buyer, and would be grateful if she'd arrange for the removal of the furniture.

'That was quick. I'll go on Monday morning. I'll probably have to stay for a couple of days,' she said apologetically to Pru. 'There isn't much I want to keep, so I'll have to try and sell the rest.'

'Stay as long as you like,' Pru replied easily, but she eventually admitted that she was concerned. Although no more attempts seemed to have been made to attack Sophie, might she be more vulnerable in London?

It didn't help when she suggested it. Sophie refused to discuss what she termed scare stories, and might even be contrary enough to take undue risks if she thought

Pru, with her two years' seniority, was nannying her.

The first chance she could get to the phone in private, on Friday afternoon, Pru rang Luke Despard.

'I'm worried in case they try something when she's on her own,' she said when she'd explained. 'Can you keep an eye on her? Without letting her know I put you up to it?'

'Of course I will. When will Sophie be around? I'll phone back.'

They were clearing away supper when he rang. Pru slipped out of the room, and when she returned ten minutes later Sophie was standing at the sink, her cheeks faintly pink, scrubbing energetically at a saucepan. Pru forbore to point out that it was actually a clean one, left draining after lunch.

'Who was it?' she asked casually. 'Someone for lessons?'

'No. No, it wasn't business. Pru—' Sophie stopped, and with extra care placed the pan on the draining board. 'It was that nice journalist, Luke Despard. He rang to ask if I'd be in London soon. Wasn't that strange, when I'll be there next week?'

'And?' Pru suppressed a smile.

'Oh, he suggested supper one evening,' Sophie said with elaborate unconcern.

'Good, you'll be busy during the day, and a bit of company in the evenings will do you good. Do you think that poulticing on the grey gelding is working, or should we call the vet?' she went on. It wouldn't do to let Sophie dwell on the apparent coincidence of Luke's call. She was too intelligent, and if she had time to think clearly she might begin to imagine things. Correct things.

She might even begin to imagine things herself, she thought with an inward smile when she saw Sophie stagger down the stairs with two suitcases. Normally she confined her luggage to a small tote bag even for several days away.

'I thought there might be some more things I could bring back with me,' Sophie said defensively, and Pru nodded, pretending not to notice the cases were considerably too heavy to be empty.

'Ring me tonight,' she said easily. 'I'm still a bit worried about that gelding's hock, might want to talk over calling the vet.'

Sophie nodded, loaded her suitcases into the boot, and was gone.

Chapter Three

At the flat Sophie spent several hours on the phone, making arrangements for various dealers to call and offer for the paintings and better pieces of furniture, and the hundreds of books her aunt had amassed.

During a lull, when she was drinking coffee and eating the sandwiches she'd brought with her for lunch, the phone rang. She swallowed hastily. Was it one of the dealers, changing the arrangements, or Pru, with some problem, or—and her heart sank—Luke to say he couldn't manage this evening?

'Hello?' she said cautiously.

A voice she didn't recognise asked curtly if that was Sophie Stein.

'Sophie Stone, yes,' she replied firmly.

'You won't hide under a stone from us,' the voice said, and raucous laughter burst into Sophie's ears. 'Like beetles and other nasty crawly things.'

'Who is that?' she demanded.

'Never you mind who we are. I just thought I'd let you know we're watching you. You won't get away next time.'

She could hear the bang of the receiver being slapped down at the other end. Furious, and scared, she wondered whether to contact the police. Then she remembered the 'last call' facility and dialled 1471 with trembling fingers. No number was recorded. They'd blocked it, whoever they were. How did they know where she was, or her aunt's telephone number? Aunt Meg had been ex-directory, and only her aunt's friends, and business contacts, plus the dealers she'd contacted, and Luke and Pru, knew it.

She tried to put it out of her mind as she spent the afternoon going through her aunt's books, and helping the librarian from the art college who had bid for them pack them into boxes and load them into his ancient van. It was seven o'clock before she was finished and able to ring Pru.

'Don't worry, it's quiet here, we're coping without you,' Pru reassured her. 'Caroline's very experienced, and works hard. And she's very patient with the nervous pupils.'

'What about that hock?'

'Better, I think. By tomorrow it should be clear. But we had a call from someone who wants us to take four horses. A Mr Stanley.'

'Four? But we haven't the space, there's only two boxes empty.'

'No, but he's adamant he wants them together. He's planning to move to the area, and after he's settled there could be another two, belonging to his kids.'

'I suppose we could convert the other barn for our own horses,' Sophie said slowly. 'It's what we intended in the long term, if things went well. And we've already got planning permission. But is it wise to rely on one person for so much custom? What if we went ahead with the expense and he changed his mind?'

'The riding school horses are outside for another couple of months, we could manage. Shall I get the builder to give me an estimate, and we can have a word tomorrow? This man wants an answer by Wednesday.'

'Do you want me to come back?' Sophie was reluctant. It would mean cancelling appointments it had taken her half a day to arrange. She didn't admit to herself she would also be sorry to miss the chance of

61

seeing Luke Despard.

'There's no need, I can get the builder here. Besides, aren't you going out with Luke tonight?'

'Yes,' Sophie said, 'but he'll understand.'

'I wouldn't dream of spoiling your evening. And no doubt you've got all sorts of dealers coming tomorrow.'

'It would be difficult to cancel, and only mean I'd have it all to do another time,' Sophie said. 'I don't want to have to stay here longer than necessary. I want to be over and done with it.'

'Then stay. But I'll have to speak to you tomorrow before agreeing with Mr Stanley. Ring me about the same time?'

Sophie had to hurry. She was meeting Luke at eight, and still had to shower and dress, as well as find her way to South Kensington. Luckily the flat was only a few minutes from the tube, and it was only four stops and a short walk to the restaurant Luke had suggested.

As she towelled herself dry she began to wish she'd agreed to his suggestion of collecting her in the car. She didn't really know why she'd refused. A sense of independence, she supposed, and unwillingness to let it appear they were more than mere acquaintances. He was being kind to her, that was all. Having become involved in her affairs when he foiled the madman in the Volvo, he seemed to feel protective towards her. It was a comforting feeling, though. Sophie had been brought up believing in female equality, and most of her friends had opted to enter once male-dominated professions such as the law, business and medicine. She had abandoned all thought of university when her grandfather had been ill so much for the last year of her schooling, and gone to help him. She hadn't wanted any other career, just had a vague feeling that a few years at university would be pleasant, and the loss hadn't affected her a great deal. If she hadn't wanted to run the stables she'd have been there with the rest of them, fighting the battles for equal rights. Nonetheless, Luke's attitude that she needed a man occasionally, to take care of situations where she wasn't physically strong enough to manage by herself, gave her a feeling of warmth.

'Be damned to women's lib!' she muttered as she slipped into her best underclothes. She glanced at the clock by the bed and tried to hurry. She'd not meant to spend so long in the bath. It would be better to take a taxi. By now there might not be many trains, and there was a change to make at Notting Hill Gate. She didn't want to be late.

In between her phone calls, or while she was waiting to be connected, she'd agonised over what to wear. Should it be the plain white and navy dress she'd worn at various formal village do's, or the pale green one she kept for invitations to drinks or dinner, the favourite methods of entertaining in the neighbourhood. Luke had already seen that, she recalled, and both were staid and unexciting, and she felt neither was suitable for dining with Luke.

She so rarely went out, and almost never to parties, that she had little else. Almost all her clothes, apart from those she wore when working in the stables, were plain and utilitarian. She had one long evening dress, bought for a formal dinner organised by a charity for rescuing abandoned horses, but that would hardly do for a little restaurant in South Kensington. Nor would the long thick woollen skirt she wore for warmth on winter evenings. Despite the central heating she and Pru had installed when they'd refurbished the property the old house had some chilly spots, especially in the drawing room where they entertained their more important business guests.

Eventually she chose a bright fuchsia pink sleeveless dress with a cream linen jacket. She'd bought the outfit for a wedding two months earlier, and never expected to wear it again. Her lifestyle didn't call for such clothes. But she was thankful she had something good to wear this evening.

As she approached the junction she saw the lights were against her and slowed down. A man sitting on a motorbike revved the engine as she passed, and she wondered why he didn't go while the lights were in his favour, if he was in such a hurry. As she waited to cross Holland Park Avenue, she glanced at her watch. It was already a quarter to eight. As well as dawdling in the bath she'd spent far longer than she'd meant to fiddling with her hair, which was too short to do anything exciting with, and then being in a hurry she'd laddered her tights and had to change them. She saw a taxi approaching on the far side of the road, and hoped the lights would change and she'd be able to get across before it passed her.

The lights changed, Sophie breathed a sigh of relief and began to cross. As she stepped off the pavement someone in a bright green and purple track suit overtook her, brushing her shoulder, and Sophie staggered, slipping on her unusually high heels as she moved sideways. She heard the roar of a powerful motorbike, then shouts, and would have fallen had a hand not grabbed at her arm and steadied her.

Out of the corner of her eye Sophie saw a motorbike hurtling down the road.

'You bloody road hog!' The voice was close to her ear, and Sophie twisted round to find a tall, abnormally thin elderly man beside her, holding her arm in a fierce grip.

'Thanks!' she gasped. 'Did he shoot the lights? I never even saw him coming.'

'He was waiting round the corner, I passed him a moment back. He didn't move until the lights were against him, and then he shot round the corner, ignoring the lights, and flashed between us with inches to spare,' the man in the tracksuit said angrily. 'You OK?'

Sophie nodded and he turned to run on. So short a time had elapsed the lights were still with him. It must have been the motorcyclist she'd seen herself. What had he been playing at? Then she remembered the threatening phone call, and shivered.

'Are you really all right? You look very pale.'

'I'm fine, really,' she managed.

'If you hadn't tripped he'd have run you over!' the older man said, and Sophie realised he was still grasping her arm.

'I'm fine. It was that jogger pushing by made me slip.'

'Fortunate for you he did,' her rescuer remarked. 'Pity I didn't get the number. And he was got up in black, like most of those maniacs seem to wear. Blast! Now the lights have changed again.'

'I was looking for a taxi,' Sophie explained. 'Here's one.' She flagged one coming across the junction. 'Can I give you a lift anywhere?'

'I live just the other side of the main road, thanks. Now sure you're all right? No twisted ankle?' He fussed about her as she got into the taxi and gave the address of the restaurant. As they drove away Sophie glanced back and saw him watching with what seemed a very intent gaze. It had all happened so swiftly she hadn't had time to be frightened, but now she began to shake. It had been a near shave. Living in the country had made her unused to London traffic. She, who had lived in New York as a child, and spent several holidays in Rome, ought to be able to cope with the craziest idiots on the roads.

She paid off the taxi, glanced around to see if Luke was there, and began to cross the narrow street towards the restaurant. He wasn't waiting for her, but the head waiter explained he'd rung to say he'd be a few minutes late, and asked what she'd drink while she was waiting.

'I'll have sherry please, dry.'

She'd have liked something stronger, but it looked a rather superior restaurant, and she didn't want to risk spoiling the taste of the food by swigging spirits. She sat in the small lounge bar, trying not to feel conspicuous on her own, and evading the enquiring glances of two men who came in shortly after her. When Luke appeared, rather dishevelled and breathless, five minutes later, she greeted him more warmly than she'd intended, and promptly blushed a fiery red. She'd meant to be cool and distant. She couldn't bear him to think she was so eager to see him. Her normal suspicious wariness had reasserted itself during the previous few days, and she was questioning why Luke was so attentive. He was bound to know all about her father. Even though he worked in a different area, and wasn't a news reporter, he couldn't help know the main facts.

'Sorry, it took me ages to find a parking space,' he apologised. 'You have a drink. Good. You look gorgeous,' he added quietly, and her fading blush returned. 'Shall we go in if our table's ready?'

Until the main course had been eaten Luke didn't mention the apparent attempts on Sophie. He talked about his work, and entertained her with accounts of some of his trips abroad when researching travel articles. She gradually relaxed and began to enjoy the evening.

When they'd chosen from the sweet trolley he asked her whether Bob or the police had discovered anything about strange cars. 'I don't suppose anyone would take much notice of a parked car, even though there are no houses near the entrance to that track.'

Sophie frowned. 'Everything's been normal, but Pru's fussing like a mother hen,' she muttered. 'I can't believe anyone would

want to try and kidnap me. It's ridiculous.'
Briefly she thought of the man on the
motorbike, but dismissed the notion. That
had been a stupid accident. He could
scarcely have dragged her across his saddle
and ridden off with her. 'What could they
gain?'

'A ransom. Crispins must be worth a lot
of money.'

'Hardly enough to make the risk worth
the danger to them.'

'Then they may be trying to kill you.
The man in the Volvo could have been
trying to make it look like an accident.
If they kidnapped you they could still
be intending to kill you later, and again
perhaps try to make it seem accidental.'

'But who would benefit?' she asked.

'If you have no enemies, or jealous rivals,
it must be for money. Are you rich?'

To his surprise she flushed again. 'I own
Crispins, and the money my aunt's flat will
fetch,' she snapped. 'I suppose that seems
a fortune to some people, but it's hardly
enough to kill me for.'

'And your father's money?' he suggested.

'If that were the reason, it would
implicate one of my family, wouldn't it?'
She pushed away her uneaten meringue. 'I

think I'd like to go now.'

Luke shook his head gently. 'I don't mean to be offensive, Sophie, but I don't know your family. It's just one possible explanation. Eat that pavlova and tell me about them. Are your parents still alive?'

Sophie stared at him for a moment and he couldn't read the expression in her eyes. Then she picked up her spoon and shrugged. 'It's rather complicated,' she said, sighing, then suddenly grinned. 'If you're planning to investigate all my extended family, I wish you luck!'

'Try me.'

She took a deep breath. 'My father was Peter Stein. But you knew that. Didn't you?'

'The writer? No, I didn't know.'

'Then why did you mention his money?'

'Just a generalisation. Most parents leave their children something.'

Sophie looked hard at him, then relaxed. 'Yes. You know his books?'

'Of course I do. They're famous.'

'He was married three times. He had a son Rod by his first wife, Arlene, but she's married again and has another son and daughter, Ben and Rita. They all live in New York. Her second husband was

71

married before and had two sons, but I
never met them. Riccardo and Guido, or
Guilio, I think. My mother was Peter's
second wife, but they only had me. After
the divorce she came back to Britain and
changed her name to Stone.'

'To avoid the connection?' he asked.

'Yes. And the publicity that went with
it. I've done the same, though of course
most of our acquaintances know.'

'Then?' he prompted.

'Then she married again and lived in
Scotland. She and Iain had no more
children. They were killed in a car smash
six years ago. Peter's third wife was Karen,
she's German, and they had a son Gerard.
She went back to Germany and married
again, and also had a son and daughter,
Helmut and Trudi. I never hear more than
a Christmas card now, but I liked her
when she was married to my father. She
was kind. Arlene was always bad-tempered
when I saw her.'

Luke grinned. 'I'll need a family tree. So
your father was Peter Stein, the writer who
was killed several years ago. It was always
assumed he was killed by some criminal
whose past he was investigating.'

Sophie nodded. 'I was only five, I barely

72

remembered it, or even him.'

'I hadn't realised. I heard about it, of course, but I was only twelve or so. I hadn't come across his books then. I know them now, the thrillers and the biographies of crooks and terrorists, but nothing about his family.'

Sophie looked at him curiously. 'He and Mom split up when I was three. Gerard wasn't born when he was killed.'

'Your grandfather, who left you the stables, was your mother's father then?'

'Yes. He always meant to, leave me Crispins. He said Mom was rich enough, her new husband, Iain Gordon, owned a distillery, and he wanted someone who'd keep the stables on, not sell out. My aunt, or rather great-aunt, who's just died, was his sister, and she never married.'

'How old are all your half-siblings?'

'I'm twenty-two, Gerard is seventeen, and Karen's other children are just fourteen and thirteen. Rod's three years older than me, and Arlene's other children, Ben and Rita Ross, are twenty-two and twenty. Tony Ross's older sons must be about twenty-seven or twenty-six.'

'I think we can count out Helmut and Trudi, they're too young. But the others are all old enough to do mischief.'

'But why should they want to kidnap me?' Sophie demanded, returning to the puzzle.

'As I said, ransom or murder. Who would inherit Crispins? Have you made a will?'

Sophie looked pale, at last beginning to accept the possibility that someone wanted her dead. She recalled the motorbike. Surely that had been an accident!

'Pru put up some money,' she said slowly, 'the amount she got from her husband's house and insurance, and I believe she borrowed a bit from her brother John, though he's far from affluent. The partnership agreement gives either of us the other one's share in the stables if one of us dies. You're not suggesting she has a motive, are you?'

'It seems unlikely, unless she has a murderous boyfriend.'

Sophie shook her head. 'There's only Guy. You saw him. But she only met him in January when they were skiing, and I don't know how serious it is.'

Luke nodded. Sophie was getting restless again. All this speculation clearly disturbed her. She didn't want to think such evil of anyone. 'The rest of your money, from your aunt, and presumably from your parents, who'd get that?'

'The money from Mom's in trust until I'm twenty-five. I made a will when she died, leaving it to a distant cousin, but I haven't seen her for years. She was Mom's only relative.'

'Not to your brothers?'

'They're half-brothers. They'll have Dad's money. But neither of them is even in this country! Rod's in New York, he works in a bank. And Gerard's still at school. They'd hardly try to kill me! Luke, it's been great seeing you, but I have dealers coming from eight tomorrow morning. I must go back to the flat.'

'My car's parked nearby. Are you free tomorrow evening, or are the dealers coming late as well?'

'I'm going to see an old school friend in the afternoon. I'm not sure what time I'll leave her.'

They drove home and Sophie was silent. Had he interpreted that as a rebuff? She thought of the lonely flat and the threatening phone call, and suddenly didn't want to be alone. Yet she could hardly ask Luke to come in without giving him the wrong impression.

'I'll ring you,' Luke said, stopping the car outside Sophie's flat, in a small two-storey block set well back from the road. He stretched a hand to cover hers and leaned slightly towards her. Sophie shrank away and hurriedly opened the door to get out. Suddenly Luke grasped her wrist and held her back. 'Who's that, near the door?' he asked quietly. 'It looks like someone trying to be inconspicuous.'

Sophie gulped. 'I can't see his face,' she whispered.

'Shall I come up with you, make sure everything's OK?'

She nodded, and they went towards the door together, Luke with his arm slipped round Sophie's waist. The man faded away round the corner of the block, and Sophie unlocked the door. When she let them into her flat Luke went first, swiftly searched all the rooms, and then declared it was all clear.

'You still look terrified,' he said, taking her hand and drawing her to sit on a big squashy settee. 'Has anything else happened?'

'It—I thought it was an accident,' she said, suddenly determined to tell him. She told him about the motorcyclist and he hugged her to him. It was so comforting to share her fears. 'After the phone call—'

'What phone call?'

'This morning. Here.' She tried to remember the exact words. 'I don't know how anyone knew I was here, or had the number.'

'Sophie, this is getting serious. We might dismiss everything else as chance, mistakes, accidents, but not a phone call threatening you. Pack your bag and come and stay in my flat.'

'No. I won't give in to them.'

'Then I'll sleep here, on this settee. Oh, Sophie, you're so stubborn!' he exclaimed, and pulled her to him. Sophie went willingly, and for a time forgot her problems as she revelled in his kisses. No other man had kissed her like this, evoking a response so fierce she never wanted to let him go. Then he gently pushed her away.

'Luke?' she asked dreamily, staring up into his eyes. 'What is it? Why have you stopped?'

'Because if I don't you won't get any sleep tonight,' he said brusquely. 'Go to bed, or I'll take you there myself, and we'd both regret that later.'

Sophie obeyed, but still spent a sleepless night veering from longing for Luke to be with her and doubts about his motives. She'd kept men at a distance for too long to change suddenly, and although her body told her she wanted him, her cautious brain insisted on suspecting him. In the morning she was so sleepy she barely noticed his departure, and promise to phone her later.

* * * *

Sophie returned home without seeing Luke again. She'd done most of the business with the dealers the following day, and after meeting her friend spent one further morning at the flat before driving home that afternoon. She'd avoided answering the phone, listening instead to the answering machine. Luke had called twice, both times asking her to call back, but she didn't respond until she was back at home, when she rang and left a message on his machine, grateful that she didn't have to talk to him direct, and parry questions about why she'd avoided his calls in London.

'Why are you avoiding him?' Pru asked.

78

'Is he like all the rest, only wanting your money?'

Sophie sighed. 'I just don't know. He said he hadn't realised who my father was.'

'Did you believe him?'

'He knew his books, but said he didn't know anything about his family. I suppose that's possible. I'm so used to having people know and ask me about him I assume everyone knows all about us.'

'He could just be cleverer than the rest,' Pru said slowly. 'Pretending not to know would put you off your guard.'

'Luke's not like that!'

Pru smiled. 'You know him so well? After three meetings? Sophie, if you trust him as much as you say, why not answer his phone messages? Why be evasive?'

'I don't know. I'm nervous, I suppose.'

'There must be some subconscious reason why you're acting like this. Do you trust him?'

'I've no reason not to.'

'It was odd the way he followed that idiot roadhog. Most people would have ignored two cars speeding round the lanes at that time of the morning.'

'He said he'd seen my face in the

lights, and I looked terrified. That's why he followed.'

'Easy to say. Is it possible he was connected to the man who chased you, and came in to rescue you so as to get into your favour?'

Sophie stared at her in amazement. 'That's hardly likely,' she protested. 'His car was damaged.'

'Only a scratch. An accomplice wouldn't do real damage. It could have been the good guy bad guy routine, one frightens you and the other seems an angel in comparison, so that you let down your guard.'

Vehemently Sophie shook her head. She couldn't accept that Luke might be so duplicitous. She went out to the stables, working herself into a state of exhaustion, knowing that unless she did she would not sleep that night.

★ ★ ★ ★

The police came the following day to ask more questions. They had discovered nothing about the ownership of the machete and shotgun, and the recovered Volvo had been wiped clean of fingerprints.

'That indicates someone with a record, not a casual joyrider,' Detective Sergeant Pickford told her. 'We can't find any trace of a strange car in the village the day they tried to abduct you, either. We've no leads at all. Has anything else suspicious happened?'

Sophie hesitated, then decided there was no harm in mentioning the phone call and the motorbike incident. She left out the lurking figure by the flat, since he'd gone and need not have had anything to do with her. As she explained what had happened Pru exclaimed in dismay, and when the detective had gone, convinced that she knew nothing to help identify the culprit, she rounded on Sophie angrily.

'Why didn't you tell me?'

'It was nothing, just an ordinary mishap, and I wasn't hurt,' Sophie protested.

'You little idiot! Don't you realise it could have been another attempt on you?' She was silent for a while. 'You were on your way to the restaurant? How long did it take?'

'Not long. Ten minutes, perhaps? I was late, but I didn't notice how much, I was just glad I hadn't kept Luke waiting. He was five minutes after me. He had a problem parking the car. He said afterwards he'd been determined to get as close to the restaurant as possible.'

Pru looked thoughtful. 'Sophie, God knows I don't want to make you more suspicious than you already are of men, but Luke is always nearby when these accidents happen. He was behind that Volvo—'

'That was pure chance,' Sophie interrupted.

'He was here early, very early, the morning those men attacked you,' Pru went on slowly. 'I always found that a bit suspicious. Why leave his hotel too early for breakfast? He could have parked somewhere away from the village, waiting for them, to tell them where you usually ride. He might even have been one of them.'

'No!' Sophie protested, distressed. 'They weren't as tall as Luke, and they were both stockier.'

'You can't be sure, not when you were surprised by the attack. Are you going to check what time he left the Randolph?' Pru demanded.

'I don't need to! I know he didn't do it!' Sophie was getting angry. 'Besides, he wasn't there, he stayed that night with some friends, and they were leaving early for the airport. He told me their flight had been delayed after all, when we were in London.'

Pru went on, disregarding Sophie's angry tone. 'And now he was late meeting you after a motorbike nearly knocked you down. It wouldn't have taken him so long to reach the restaurant on a bike, and park it, then take off his leathers and dump them in his car, parked there earlier. Or he could even have gone home and collected his car from there if it was on his way. Is it?'

'Near enough. But I can't believe it!' Sophie protested. 'I'll grant the others look like kidnap attempts, but this would have been murder! It must have been an accident! And Luke's never said he has a bike.'

'That doesn't prove anything. And who else wants you dead?' Pru asked brutally.

'But why should Luke want mc dead?' Sophie demanded. 'If it's true, what you're insinuating, that he's after my money, then surely he'd want me alive. I wouldn't be much use to him in a morgue!'

'Look, Sophie, the only people to benefit from your death, the way your father left his money, are your half-brothers. How can you know Luke isn't working for one of them while they're safely fixing alibis at home?'

'I won't listen to you any more!' Sophie raged. 'Surely there's enough for all of us? Rod and Gerard can't want my share as well. The only person who'd really benefit would be you! Yes, you, Pru Bailey! You'd get my half of Crispins. It isn't worth millions, but then you're not used to millions, are you? A few hundred thousand would be enough, with me out of the way, so that you could own it all. Did you plot this because I'd have nothing to do with John? Then you could both enjoy it. That would be a long way up for village kids born in a tied cottage, children of a farm labourer, wouldn't it?'

She stormed out of the kitchen, locked herself into her bedroom, and ignored Pru's knocks on the door. She hardly slept, seeing Pru's hurt look all night, and by morning hated herself for her loss of control. Rising early she made a cup of tea and took a tray up to Pru's room.

'Pru, I'm so dreadfully ashamed of myself,' she said when she'd set it down on the table beside the bed. 'I didn't mean it. I was a prize bitch. I can't expect you to forgive me, but I wanted you to know I'll never forgive myself for the dreadful things I said.'

Pru sat up in bed. 'I understand, Sophie,' she said quietly. 'You've been under a lot of strain, and I made it worse by trying to make you suspicious of Luke. I'm sure he isn't trying to kill you, it's ridiculous, but I'm so worried for you. I was just trying out every possibility. Do you want to buy me out, dissolve our partnership?'

Sophie bit her lip. 'No, of course I don't. But do you want to leave? I wouldn't be surprised after what I said.'

Pru smiled then. 'I can't imagine any other life,' she said in a low voice. 'I can forget it if you can. And I promise never to try and cast suspicion on Luke again.'

Chapter Four

The next two weeks seemed endless to Sophie. Although Pru made a valiant effort to smile whenever they were together, and said nothing about Sophie's outburst, she was clearly unhappy. She moved around with far less than her normal exuberance, her expression grave when she thought Sophie wasn't looking, and she found excuses to go out, supposedly visiting friends, when work for the day was finished.

Sophie had tried to apologise again that first evening, but Pru, blinking hard, had turned away and shaken her head.

'Don't, Sophie, it's all over, I want to forget.'

'Would you like to go away, have a holiday?' Sophie asked tentatively, hoping Pru wouldn't interpret this as a desire to see her out of the way.

Pru shook her head. 'I had a fortnight skiing in January,' she reminded Sophie, 'and another week in May, at Guy's home.' Briefly she smiled, and then shrugged. 'I can't be with him. He's away training those wretched pilots,' she added. 'I don't want to be on my own, I'd rather work. Then I don't have time to think.'

Sophie tried to keep out of Pru's way as much as she could, arranging lessons which took her out onto the bridleways while Pru was working in the paddocks or stables, but they couldn't avoid one another in the house. It was a relief that Bob began to drop by at lunch time, and they could chat to him while they drank soup or ate sandwiches, all they normally stopped for then.

'Have you heard from Luke Despard?' Bob asked one day, about a week after the quarrel.

'He's rung a couple of times,' Sophie said and glanced at Pru. The calls had come in the evenings when Pru was out, and she hadn't mentioned them.

Pru lifted her eyebrows and then, aware of her dubious expression, smiled brightly. Sophie cringed inwardly. It was almost worse having Pru being so patently insincere than arguing about Luke's motives.

'Good chap, Luke,' Bob went on, oblivious to this byplay. 'He asked me to let him know if anything untoward happened.'

'He did?' Pru asked, her tone sharp, but swiftly resumed her bright smile. It was, Sophie thought, almost a grimace, it was so false.

'I think he has a bit more than a casual interest,' Bob said, chuckling. 'But nothing has happened, has it? No more attacks. I'm hoping it was just a series of bizarre coincidences, kids fooling about. But I'm surprised Luke hasn't been down. I thought he was planning to.'

Were the threatening phone call to the flat, and the motorcyclist, just coincidences? Sophie shuddered. She wanted to think so. She had to believe this or she'd go mad looking behind her every time she took the car out, doors locked and windows tight closed even on the hottest day, scanning the tracks in front of her on every ride, and half expecting an intruder to leap out of her wardrobe every time she went into her bedroom. Although the nights were still short, now she never even stepped out to the dustbins after dark, and never rode alone in the early mornings.

Fortunately it was the school holidays and they were exceptionally busy, and as well as fitting in as many rides and lessons as they possibly could, were trying to clear the barn which was to be converted, in readiness for the builder to start the following week. She was too exhausted to lie awake for long, worrying.

Bob seemed to know the subject of Luke was a sensitive one, for he didn't press for answers, just gave Sophie the odd wink or knowing smile when he took his leave. She felt like screaming. OK, Luke was attractive, he was smooth and sophisticated, he'd travelled all over the world, met famous people, and he'd probably saved her life, but that didn't mean she was a swooning Victorian miss ready to fall into his arms and pining for him to declare undying love. But he was decidedly attractive. For the first time in years she'd almost been ready to trust a man, let down her guard, and Pru had sown doubts in her mind. She couldn't, wouldn't believe he meant to harm her, for what could there be in it for him? Pru's speculation that he was in league with one of her half brothers was too fantastic to be taken seriously. Far more likely that he wanted to marry her and her father's money.

When, on Monday two weeks later, her solicitor rang to ask whether she wanted to go to the flat again to check everything before the new owners took possession, read the meters, have a final look round, or whether she wanted him to do it, she leapt at the opportunity of a day in London.

'I'll come on Wednesday,' she said. Most of the horses had been hired for the whole day by a group of experienced riders who didn't need accompanying, and the work at the stables would be unusually light. 'There are a few small things I left there, a kettle and some crockery. I'll drop the keys into your office around midday, if that's all right.'

His office was near Lower Regent Street, she'd spend a few hours shopping, perhaps buy Pru a present, some fabulously expensive perfume.

Pru was encouraging when Sophie hesitantly explained her plans. 'Why don't you stay in town for a couple of nights?' she suggested. 'If you can't beg a bed with one of your old school friends, stay in an hotel. I can manage without you, and you could do with a break.'

Did she want to be rid of her? Sophie admitted that two or three days away, where the sight of Pru's wan face would not constantly remind her of the unforgivable words she'd uttered, was deeply attractive. But Thursday was unusually busy. She ought to be back to take her share of the work.

'I don't think I will,' she said. 'You'd find it difficult to cover my lessons on Thursday, but thanks for the suggestion.'

'Ring Luke up and suggest lunch,' Pru said, her voice taut.

Sophie looked at her. 'I can't do that. Besides, there won't be time. I was thinking of using the opportunity of getting some more riding boots and a new jacket. Mine's shabby, and there's the big show at the end of August. I can look in Harrods or Lilywhites.'

'The local shops would have what you wanted, and much cheaper,' Pru said, then added hurriedly, 'but of course you can afford the best. Go and see what London can offer.'

Sophie set off early to try and beat the daily commuters along the M40, but she found that half of them seemed to set out before seven in the morning, and once into the outskirts of London progress was slow. It was nine o'clock before she drew into the parking spaces behind her aunt's small block of flats. Once more she blessed the architects for providing each resident with a space, since battling for public parking in the streets nearby was a frustrating process. She let herself into the flat, which felt stuffy, collected the usual litter of junk mail, dropped it and her handbag on top of the kitchen units, and went round opening windows while the kettle boiled. She paused for a moment in the sitting room, overlooking the road. There was a minor traffic jam, the cars and vans stationary, and bikes weaving their way between the other vehicles. Sophie shuddered. It was so much quicker by bicycle, but the way heavy lorries thundered past pedal-bikes, within inches of the handlebars, giving no quarter, allowing no margin for the unintentional wobble, terrified her. The Fiat wasn't much protection, but she couldn't be flicked off into the path of something else just by a momentary nudge from a juggernaut.

A boy was delivering newspapers opposite, and Sophie glanced at her watch. Poor residents, having to wait for their daily dose of scandal and disaster until this late. Presumably they got it with the cornflakes during term time. She watched idly as the boy stopped to talk to a man lounging on a low wall in front of a shabby old house which seemed to have escaped redevelopment or Sixties gentrification, then turned away as she heard the click of the kettle turning itself off. How loud the sound was in the empty flat. She was leaving the curtains and carpets, but there was still a hollow echo which made her shiver slightly.

There was nowhere to sit apart from the windowsill, so Sophie took her coffee, instant, sugarless and black, but better than none at all, to the front window seat and sat there while she riffled through the mail. There were a couple of bills which the solicitor would deal with, and she put them aside. There were several envelopes promising untold wealth if only the recipient replied within a week, a couple of leaflets for local events already over, and a thick envelope which was addressed to her.

She stared at it in surprise. Why should anyone send mail for her here? Perhaps it was from one of her aunt's friends or colleagues who didn't know her other address. It was secured with sticky tape, and Sophie swore as she struggled to open it, chipping a nail in the process. At last she pulled the flap free, and drew out a small box, not much bigger than a matchbox. It had sticky tape wrapped round it, but this time Sophie was able to slide her nail beneath it under the lid and break the seal. She opened the box, and after a moment of rigid horror jerked convulsively and threw the box and contents out of the window, knocking her mug of coffee out as well.

She stood up and shook herself, feeling her skin crawl. She wasn't unduly squeamish, she could deal with spiders or worms, but one thing she hated was woodlice. The box had been full of the beastly little pests. She looked carefully around, but couldn't see any strays. Her skin was still itchy, so she went into the bathroom, stripped, and showered, thankful it was an instant heating shower, and she'd left one towel, though a small one, here. Shaking every garment before she put it on again she wondered whether she ought to go down and clear away the broken mug, but by now the woodlice would have spread all over the patch of concrete beneath the windows, and she couldn't bear the idea of finding any crawling beneath the shards of pottery. There were no children who could get hurt, and the area was full of cast-off beer cans and plastic burger boxes, plus the odd helping of discarded chips and worse. The place was swept once a week, and as Sophie leaned out of the window she judged, by the state of it, the sweeping was due any minute now.

As she stepped back she noticed the man across the road hadn't moved. Had he seen her dropping the box? For a second she felt embarrassed at her moment of panic, then shrugged. It was none of his business, and he couldn't have seen what it was she'd dropped. She'd better do what she'd come for, then she could get out of the flat, which suddenly seemed menacing.

While she read the meters and noted down the readings she was thinking about the unpleasant parcel. Was it yet another of the inexplicable accidents that had plagued her recently? She felt an urge to telephone Luke, but as she reached out for the receiver she hesitated. Who could have sent the parcel?

Suppressing her distaste she retrieved the envelope from the wastebin, and looked for a postmark. There was none, not even a smudged apology of one, and there were no stamps. It had been delivered by hand. If someone was trying to kidnap her and hold her to ransom, it could be any nutter. If their aim was to kill her it narrowed the field. Slowly she went through the list of people who could benefit by her death. It didn't seem as ridiculous now to imagine the incidents were real, not accidents. Then she told herself not to be paranoid. Pru couldn't have delivered the parcel, nor could she have driven the murderous Volvo. Luke hadn't driven the Volvo. Either of them, a small voice within her insisted, could have had an accomplice, but was that likely? Of course not.

That left her brothers, who would benefit far more financially than anyone else. She looked at the phone, and suddenly made up her mind. She rang Karen first, in Bonn. There was no reply. Her present husband, Franz, worked for the foreign ministry, and she had his number too. A polite voice, switching instantly to perfect English, informed her that Herr Hoffmann was on vacation, an extended trip to visit friends in Australia. The rest of the family would doubtless be with him. Sophie gave an unconscious sigh of relief She liked Gerard best of her two brothers.

She looked up Rod's number in her diary, and as she was about to dial paused, frantically trying to work out the time difference between London and New York. It was eleven now, she'd spent far too long dithering since she arrived at the flat. It would be six in New York, not too early. Rod had an hour's commute to work, he'd be up or almost. Or did summer time make a difference? She didn't care. She'd wake him anyway. She dialled and let the phone ring for thirty counts. He wasn't there. Of course there were all sorts of explanations, it didn't mean he was here in England trying to kill her. She then called Arlene, Rod's mother, in her summer cottage on Cape Cod, to be greeted with an abrupt 'Yes?' on the second ring.

'Arlene, it's Sophie here.'

'Sophie? What are you doing phoning so early?'

'I hope I didn't wake you?'

'No. I'm up to my eyes in packing. Left to do it all myself, of course.'

'Packing?' Sophie heard her voice squeak. 'Off on vacation?' she asked. 'I thought you always spent the summer on the Cape?'

'What's that to you? As it happens, Tony has moved to Belgium, to work at SHAPE headquarters for a year, and I'm left to close everything up here and follow him. Even Ben and Rita have decamped.'

'Have they? It was Ben I wanted to speak to, actually. Do you know where he is?'

'No. Nor Rita. They're off backpacking

97

somewhere, they don't bother to keep me informed. They'll just expect everything to be waiting for them when they get back, but this time I won't be.'

She was in such a bad mood Sophie couldn't make it worse. 'Where's Rod?' she asked, not bothering to make an excuse for asking.

'I haven't the faintest. I certainly don't poke my nose into his affairs, or I'd have it bitten off. Haven't heard from him for a month or more. Now if you've finished, I have to get on.'

Sophie replaced the receiver thoughtfully. Rod might be anywhere, so might Arlene's other two children by Tony Ross. She couldn't do any more at the flat except pack up the kettle. It was as she was closing and locking the windows that she thought she ought to have asked for Tony's address in Belgium. Unless Arlene wrote to her, which was unlikely, she wouldn't be able to get in touch except through the SHAPE switchboard. She was closing the last window, in the sitting room, when she saw the same man sitting on the wall opposite. As far as she knew he hadn't moved all morning, and she had a sudden horrid conviction he was watching her. Luckily she'd be using the back door leading to the parking places, and he wouldn't know.

Loading the boxes into the car she wanted to leap in and drive away instead of taking the tube into central London. She could post the keys to her solicitor. She didn't like being so frightened, though. She would not live the rest of her life being afraid of shadows, suspecting everyone, even her best friend. But she dreaded having to walk out from the flats and possibly confront him. She tried to persuade herself that he could be harmless. He was probably unemployed, loafing away the hours, maybe unwelcome in a bed and breakfast hostel. He might even be homeless. That made her wonder if he was spying out a possible squat, and she felt disgusted with herself and her suspicions. Despite this, it was with some relief that she recalled the narrow passageway that led from the flats between the houses behind her, a relic of more spacious days when all the houses here had back entrances. She could go that way and get to the tube station without passing the watcher. She glanced round. There was another Fiat parked here, the same colour as hers. She thought it belonged to a woman who collected her children from a nursery every day. She'd be leaving soon, and the watcher might assume Sophie had left. By the time she came back he could have gone.

Sophie almost ran down the alleyway and to the tube station. She left the keys with the solicitor, signed some final documents, and treated herself to lunch in a small restaurant in Piccadilly. She found suitable boots and a jacket, and arranged for them to be delivered. She didn't want to lug them round all afternoon, and while she was away from the stables she wanted to stay away as long as possible.

At last she had to think about returning. She had wandered up Regent Street and along Oxford Street, and her hands were full of stores' bags. Usually reluctant to buy clothes, she'd found herself buying almost compulsively, lambswool sweaters in jewel colours which suited her dark colouring, a long pleated skirt in a wool so fine it took up virtually no space. In black, it would be wonderful for winter parties, matching with anything, but she had to buy a couple of silk shirts to go with it, and some smart shoes and a pair of evening sandals. She thought of her utilitarian underwear and raided Miss Selfridge for dainty bras made mostly of lace, and minuscule briefs. Then she had to get an evening bag and some ultra-fine tights. By this time she was tempted to take a taxi, but the tube station at Marble Arch was close, and she hadn't far to walk at the other end. She'd completely forgotten the suspicious watcher.

By the time she'd bought a ticket and struggled down to the platform she was beginning to regret her decision. The rush hour had started, and the trains had been delayed, so the platform got crowded very quickly. There were a couple of young men standing in front of her and when Sophie, pushed by the people behind her, was jostled against their backs, they turned round with angry expressions. These faded as they met Sophie's apologetic look, and they moved slightly apart so that she was between them.

'I'm sorry,' she said. 'I didn't mean to shove, the people behind pushed me.'

'That's OK, darlin',' one of them said, grinning, then turned away as the sound of an approaching train came. The crowd on the platform swayed, and Sophie felt another shove in the small of her back, an insistent pressure that forced her inexorably towards the edge of the platform a step away. She cried out in fright as she felt herself falling, and the two men each grabbed an arm and hauled her back to safety.

'You don't wanna delay the trains no more, luv,' one of them said, and still holding her arms they forced a way onto the already crowded train as doors opened right in front of them.

Sophie tensed, recalling the kidnappers and how they'd held on to her until Sam and Bob had scared them off. Then she told herself not to be silly, they couldn't abduct her on a train packed solid with commuters.

'You didn't lose any bags, did you?' one was asking, and Sophie shook her head. They'd been anchored so firmly to her wrists that although they'd dragged painfully, none had slipped from her grasp.

'Thanks. I could have gone under the train,' Sophie gasped, trying to still the sudden trembling which attacked her. 'Someone pushed me again,' she said, twisting to try and look at the people who'd crammed onto the train behind them.

'Just impatient,' her other rescuer said with a shrug. 'But I think you need lookin' after. Would you like us to see you safely home? Be a pleasure, darlin'.'

Sophie laughed and shook her head. They were right. It had been no more than some impatient commuter. She wasn't used to the tube, and had been taking up a lot of room with her many parcels, so whoever had pushed might have thought there was more space than there actually was. It was ridiculous to let her crazy suspicions frighten her at every small mishap.

She tried to convince herself of this all the way back to the flat and the comparative safety of her car, but couldn't help looking over her shoulder every few yards to make sure there were no homicidal villains creeping up behind her. She reached the car safely, and didn't appreciate quite how scared she'd been until, having piled her shopping onto the rear seat, she started to get in. A hurried step behind her made her swing round in alarm, tense once more.

'Luke! You scared me! How did you know I was here?'

'I phoned Crispins, and Mrs Miller told me. I've been waiting for you for an hour. You're jumpy. Has anything else happened?'

She looked at him and wondered. 'You're always appearing just after someone's attacked me,' she said accusingly.

'What do you mean?' he asked sharply.

'It was very odd you were driving through lanes out of your way and just happened to follow me.'

'I explained how you looked frightened.'

'Then you arrived so early that day they tried to kidnap me. And you were late at the restaurant, after the motorbike nearly knocked me down.'

'Are you accusing me of trying to kill you?' he asked, incredulous. 'Sophie, darling, that's the last thing I'd do!'

'You'd be far better off marrying me first, or can't you bear the thought?'

He laughed. 'Sophie, my love, is this a proposal? If it is, I'll accept.'

'No it isn't!' she stormed at him. 'I'm sick of men wanting me for my money and what's coming to me from my father! Just as I'm sick of being attacked, and if it weren't for you I wouldn't be thinking every minor mishap's a deliberate attempt to kill me either!'

'Do be consistent! If you are in danger

you should be taking care, not accusing me of scaremongering!'

'So I'm inconsistent, am I? Next you'll be telling me I'm a stupid woman unable to look after myself!'

'You've been glad enough of my help in the past. But if you don't like it, you can do without. All I've been doing is to try and make you see sense!' he said angrily. 'You go along as if you're immune to danger, but no one is totally safe.'

He turned and marched away, and Sophie stared after him, half of her wanting to run after him, half still suspicious that his denials hadn't been convincing enough. She clambered into the car, watched as Luke's Audi swept out of the little car park, then did up the safety belt. Then she began to tremble uncontrollably. She wanted desperately to follow Luke, have him reassure her, come and protect her, and then she shook her head. If it hadn't been for his suggestions, his questions, she wouldn't be thinking these things, suspecting would-be murderers everywhere.

Sophie didn't recall much of the homeward journey. She'd sat in the car for ages, and by the time she'd forced herself to drive the worst of the rush hour traffic had gone. At home she carried in her shopping to find Pru reading a newspaper in the kitchen.

Pru eyed the bags with interest. 'Early Christmas presents?' she asked.

'No, I decided my wardrobe needed variety. I'll take these upstairs and then unload the rest.' But Luke will never see them, she thought bleakly. All that shopping was a waste of time.

'Mrs Miller left supper in the oven,' Pru said. 'Leave the rest till later. Did you do everything?'

She seemed in a better, more relaxed mood than for the past three weeks. 'Yes, everything was fine, except—' Sophie stopped abruptly. She'd almost forgotten the man and the woodlice, and she wasn't sure she wanted to talk about the incident on the tube either. And she certainly didn't want to tell Pru about her row with Luke. It would restart the argument, and if Pru now felt less aggrieved she didn't want to remind her of her earlier silly accusation.

'Except what?'

Sophie thought hurriedly. 'The flat felt so strange, empty. None of Aunt Meg's things were there, and it was so stuffy, and it was odd to think I'll never go there again.'

Pru nodded. 'I felt the same when David died and I had to sell his house. Did you see Luke?'

'No,' Sophie lied. 'I didn't intend to. You knew that.'

'He phoned here, this morning,' Pru said, 'just after you'd gone. I told him you'd be at the flat for some of the morning, and I rather got the impression he'd contact you there.'

Sophie shook her head.

'What is it?' Pru asked, and her tone was back to the normal affectionate one of the past. 'There's something else, I know.'

Sophie glanced at her, and smiled reluctantly. 'When I came here for holidays, and tried to kid you I'd groomed the horses properly, you always knew when I was being economical with the truth,' she said. 'I'm being silly, but I'm so tired of strange things happening, and some of them *are* deliberate. Even if the rest are just accidents or coincidences.'

'What accidents? Do you mean more? Come on! Sophie, tell me what you mean.'

Sophie complied, though she didn't

mention Luke. She couldn't bear the thought of Pru's obvious satisfaction if she thought they'd quarrelled. 'But it's so unlikely. People are so rude these days, they push and shove without a second thought. It doesn't even occur to them that they might be pushing somebody under a bus or a train, so long as they don't get left behind!'

'How often has it happened before?' Pru asked. 'You've been up to London a dozen times. Have you ever been pushed under a train before?'

'Of course not!'

'Someone watching the flat, perhaps. A nasty parcel, delivered by hand, deliberate nastiness. Then yet another accident? After the two attempts here? And the motorbike. It's much too frequent to be coincidence. And these aren't just kidnap attempts, Sophie,' she said angrily.

'But it's ridiculous! In the first place, why should anyone want to kill me? And how do they know where I'll be? Pru, I can't believe it, but I've been watching my back all the time the last few days. I'm getting so nervous, but the only people to benefit would be my family, and surely none of them would want to kill me!'

'Whoever it is could easily watch the flat. Luckily they won't be able to hang about here, they'd be spotted at once, so now you should be safer.'

'Do you believe I'm in danger?'

Pru looked uncomfortable. 'I don't want to, but it would be foolish to ignore what's happened.'

'There's no proof. And until there is, what can I do? Let's forget it. Was there any post for me?'

'A couple of personal letters. A few asking about lessons or livery, I left everything on the dresser.'

Sophie stood up and went across the kitchen. She stayed there while she glanced at the opened letters, then brought the unopened envelopes back to the chair. 'A wedding invitation,' she said. 'Why are all my schoolfriends suddenly getting married? That's the third this year.'

'Soon?' Pru asked.

'Next month. I don't think I'd fancy September for a wedding. Too hot.' She opened the other envelope, and Pru, idly watching, was startled to see Sophie's colour drain from her face.

'What is it?' she demanded. Sophie held out the single slip of card.

'Read it,' she said faintly. 'I was wrong, it seems.'

Pru took the card and examined it. 'It's quite short, on the back of one of those postcards they sell at art galleries, and it could be innocuous. "Sorry we missed you in London. Never mind, I'm sure we'll run into you one day soon. Happy dreams." And then it's just signed with a squiggle.'

'On the face of it the words are innocent enough, but after what's happened, the meaning's clear. Pru, now I believe that someone wants to kill me.'

Chapter Five

Sophie was distracted for the next few days. She couldn't stop thinking of Luke, going over the quarrel, analysing every word, and most of the time wishing she had not accused him of being involved in the attacks on her. She didn't believe it. Would she ever see him again? It was unlikely, he would not want to have such dreadful accusations flung at him again.

She was cleaning tack, sitting on an upturned bucket in the sunshine, when he appeared in the yard and strode across to her. Her heart leapt. In jeans and a thin black silk shirt, his blond hair gleaming in the sunlight, he looked like a Norse god. She had an overwhelming desire to throw herself into his arms, then a worm of doubt about his feelings for her crawled into her mind, and she merely nodded coldly.

'Hello. I'm on my way to Oxford, thought I'd call in and see what's been happening,' he said, and his smile was just the same as ever, though a hint of anxiety lurked at the back of his eyes.

Sophie stood up slowly. 'I'm fine, thanks. I'll just hang up this bridle.' She backed into the dimly lit tack room and the light became even dimmer as Luke stepped in after her, blocking the doorway.

'Sophie, I shouldn't have left you like that,' he said softly, and suddenly she was in his arms, he was crushing her to his chest, kissing her eyes, her nose, her cheeks, until he pulled her head up firmly and captured her lips. 'Darling, I've missed you so very much. Am I forgiven?'

'Luke! It's me that should be asking for forgiveness,' she muttered, gasping for breath beneath the hail of kisses. 'I'm sorry, I'm so sorry for the rotten things I said, I didn't mean them, I was just so frightened, feeling so alone.'

'I know, and I should have realised. Forgiven?'

She was demonstrating how much when Pru's voice, amused, interrupted them.

'Children! What a bad example to set the ponies!'

Luke laughed, and turned round, his arms still about Sophie, to face her. 'Hello, Pru.'

'What are you doing here?'

'I'm on my way to Oxford. I have to work in the Bodleian for a few days, on some special papers for one of my subjects. I decided to call in on my way.'

'Why don't you stay here? It's not that far a drive to Oxford, and you'd be more comfortable than in an hotel,' Sophie said eagerly, then looked guiltily at Pru. 'You don't mind, Pru, do you?'

'Of course not. Come along in. I'll go and get the spare room ready for you,' Pru said cheerfully. 'We'll be having lunch in half an hour, just soup and a salad.'

'Fine. I'd love to stay, and it's good of

you to ask me here. I'll take up my things. Same room?'

'And I need to finish setting up the jumps for this afternoon,' Sophie said, turning away. She suddenly felt incredibly happy. Luke wasn't a murderer! She couldn't for one moment longer believe that it was a remote possibility. The instinctive rush of pleasure she'd felt on seeing him told her that, surely. She paused, standing with a pile of wooden bricks clutched to her chest, forgetting the wall in the jumping paddock which she was supposed to be raising.

Which of her new blouses should she wear tonight? It was too warm for a sweater, but one of the silk shirts would be ideal. The long skirt would be too warm too, and perhaps overdoing it, but she had a short white denim skirt which showed off her long legs, and the peacock blue shirt, with her mother's gold chain and the diamond earrings she seldom wore... Sophie snatched back her thoughts and began to pile the bricks along the top of the wall. That was far too much over the top, gold and diamond jewellery. Pru's already lively suspicions that she had fallen for the handsome Luke Despard would be confirmed. And she hadn't. She didn't make a habit of falling for men. Not any men, her thoughts amended. As she raised the bars on the other jumps she tried to analyse her feelings for Luke. He was devastatingly attractive, and sheer animal lust would make many girls fall for him. Perhaps that was all she felt? Also, he'd probably saved her life when they'd first met, and that would make her grateful. St George and the Dragon syndrome. Rescued heroines automatically fell for their rescuers, didn't they?

Angrily Sophie heaved some more brushwood to repair one of the fences that seemed to flummox most riders, and as a result looked like an anaemic hedge regularly attacked by a stampeding herd of buffalo. It had to be renewed on a weekly basis. Of course she wasn't in love with Luke. It was ridiculous. Then why had she bought all those new clothes, suitable for wearing when out with him, but impossible for evenings at home?

She sighed, checking the jumps. They were all ready, and Pru was calling her for lunch. She'd have to go and face him, and she was no nearer deciding on her attitude. It had been going out with Luke which had made her aware of the limitations of her wardrobe, yes, she'd concede that, but it didn't follow the new clothes were meant for him.

Pru talked brightly during lunch, asking Luke about his work, but when she'd made coffee she said she needed to check something outside and would skip it. Sophie took a deep breath, poured out two cups, and took Luke's to where he'd flopped into one of the armchairs.

'I could sleep here, it's so comfortable,' he sighed. 'I was up half the night, finishing off what I had to do before I could get away.' She smiled down at him and he went on, 'Sophie, come and sit down. I can't talk with you looming over me. Pru asked me to have a word with you.'

Sophie sighed. 'What about? It's bad enough having Pru fussing round me, nagging me to take more precautions, without you starting too.'

'Sophie, you've got to consider this seriously!'

She sat facing him, and sipped her coffee. 'I do, Luke. But I can't and won't believe my family may be out to kill me.'

'Someone is,' he said bluntly. 'Have

you told the police about all these other attacks?'

'They know about the man in the Volvo, and the poison pen letter. I told them about the motorbike too, but it seemed such a feeble suspicion. The woodlice were nasty, but could have been a childish trick.'

'What woodlice?' He asked sharply.

'I was sent a parcel of them, at the flat.' Sophie shuddered. 'I know it's feeble of me, but I can't bear them!' she added rather shamefacedly. 'It's only them, I don't mind other insects, but somehow they give me the shivers.'

He reached out and held her hand. 'My poor sweet, how horrible. How did they come? By post?'

'No, there were no post marks or stamps.'

'It has to be someone who knows you hate them.'

'Most people probably feel squeamish,' Sophie said. 'Let's forget them! Everything else could have been an accident. If I went to the police again they'd think I was paranoid. And what could they do? I couldn't have a bodyguard all the time.'

'The men trying to kidnap you wasn't

an accident. That was deliberate.'

'Yes, but it might have been against the stables, not me, like that time the livery horses were let out.'

'The mysterious Tricia. Have you heard any more of her?'

Sophie shook her head. 'Nothing.'

'These accidents might have been just that, but combined with the deliberate malice that seems to be about, I don't accept they are accidents. Your family and Pru have the best motives.'

'Not Pru. How can you suggest it? Anyway she was here while I was in London, she couldn't have had anything to do with it.'

'She might have had an accomplice.'

Sophie shook her head. 'That's melodramatic, Luke! We had a row when she was trying to persuade me it was—' she paused, '—well, someone else, and I was beastly to her. She was so hurt, I can't believe she can be wishing me harm. And after all, half the value of this place isn't very much.'

'It would be a vast fortune for most young women,' Luke said, amused. 'Property round here is expensive.'

'It can't be Pru.' Sophie was adamant,

her eyes stormy, her lips compressed.

'Then your half-brothers? Do you know where they are?'

Sophie breathed deeply, trying to regain the temper she'd nearly lost. She had to admit she'd tried to contact them. 'Gerard's family are in Australia, and I think Rod's away,' she said reluctantly. 'His mother is moving to Belgium. The rest of the family are on vacation, but I don't know where.' She explained all she'd managed to discover.

'Ring Rod again now.'

'He'll be at work.'

'Where?'

'New York. He works at an investment bank.'

'Do you have the number?'

'No, just the name, but I think there's only one branch.'

Luke reached for the telephone. 'I'll get the number from International Enquiries. What's the name?'

Ten minutes later he replaced the receiver. 'Rod is on vacation too. She doesn't know him personally, but she looked up the roster for me. He began it on Monday, just for this week, and then he's due to go on a course, but the girl didn't know where and wasn't prepared to find out.'

'He couldn't have been here all this time, then,' Sophie pointed out, relieved. 'And Gerard is a schoolboy, and Rod's other brother isn't much older. It can't be them.'

She refused to accept any more arguments, saying she had to take a class, and Luke snatched an hour's sleep. Out of perversity Sophie rejected her new clothes when she changed for dinner, and pulled out an old, faded summer dress she'd last worn at school. She considered her reflection with some satisfaction. A pale pink, with high neck and demurely gathered skirt, it made her look about sixteen. No one, least of all Luke, could suspect she was dressing for him. She didn't want to give the wrong impression. No doubt he was concerned, having seen the start of what she was beginning, secretly, to accept as some sort of dangerous persecution. It went no further, though. Yet he was a journalist. And through her father's reputation she was newsworthy. Perhaps he saw a story in all this, some exclusive he could capitalise on. Well, she wouldn't make the mistake of thinking his interest in her was personal, whatever he said.

At dinner Pru did most of the talking. Luke seemed slightly amused at her questions, but answered them readily enough. Sophie contributed little, until they had moved to sit in the large drawing room full of old-fashioned furniture unchanged since Sophie's grandmother's day. Then Pru made another excuse and vanished.

'Now you can't escape, and I want to know every detail of every single attack,' Luke said.

Sophie looked at him, and noted the determination in his eyes. She sighed. 'OK, but it won't help. I don't know much.'

Luke had a small tape recorder which he switched on. 'Let's start with the car chase.' He took her through every incident, probing for details Sophie had forgotten. But at the end he had to confess that there were no significant clues.

'How long can you stay here?' Sophie asked.

'A few days, unless you throw me out. I have some work to do in the Bodleian Library in Oxford.'

'I thought you had to have tickets to read there?'

'I have one, I was at Magdelen.'

'I don't know anything about you,' Sophie discovered. 'You know all my family's guilty secrets and I haven't a clue about yours.'

'It's getting late. Come out for dinner with me tomorrow and I'll reveal all.'

'We can't desert Pru,' Sophie said hurriedly, though she had flushed slightly and hoped Luke couldn't detect her suddenly racing heart.

'Pru won't mind, and even if she did, would you care? She's not your keeper. You don't have to ask her permission.'

Was he protesting too much? Sophie shrugged off her doubts. She'd enjoyed their meal in London, despite the motorbike incident, and, she thought with a sudden thrill of anticipation, she could wear one of her new silk shirts. 'Thanks, then. I'd like that.'

He stood up, and Sophie scrambled to her feet. When he smiled at her like that, his dark eyes looking at her so intently, her heart did all sorts of crazy things. She wanted him to kiss her again, as he had at the flat. Then, as he crossed the short space which divided them and lifted his hand towards her face, the unreliable organ began pounding so loudly she was sure he'd hear it. His fingers, warm and soft, touched her cheek fleetingly, he bent and brushed her hair with his lips, and while she was still savouring the delight of his closeness and waiting for his warmer kisses he moved quickly away. When she opened her eyes he had left the room.

Sophie's own hand crept up to where her cheek still tingled. She sighed deeply, feeling stranded. Then, hearing Pru's footsteps in the kitchen she fled for the stairs. Pru mustn't see her like this. Every cell of her body would give her away. She felt as though she was a glowing, radiating being. How crazy, she thought, her hand still on her cheek when she climbed into bed, as if to capture Luke's touch, to feel so ridiculously happy, enchanted even, just because of a casual caress. But it wasn't enough, she wanted more. She doubted whether she'd close her eyes that night, thinking about it, but within seconds she'd drifted into a dreamless sleep, and woke more refreshed than she had been since the whole nightmare had begun.

★ ★ ★ ★

When Luke came down for breakfast he told Sophie he'd been listening to the tape, making notes, but nothing new had occurred to him. Pru was determinedly cheerful, although Sophie caught her once or twice casting worried looks at Luke. She said nothing, however, and soon went out to the stables. Before Sophie could follow Bob Jenkins came in, Sam prancing at his heels.

'Hello, Luke, I thought that was your car outside. Glad to see you again. Have you come to keep an eye on Sophie?'

'I'm sure you do that.'

'I heard what had happened in London. That was worrying. I try to walk round the bridlepaths every day or so, but I don't think they'll try abducting her again,' Bob said. 'Sophie doesn't ride on her own in the early mornings now, do you, but she insists she has to go out alone occasionally.'

'If I didn't I'd go mad,' Sophie put in.

'From what we know they're trying different methods each time. That makes it difficult to be prepared.'

'You're more at risk in London, on your own,' Luke said. 'We can watch more easily here and try to catch whoever it is.'

'It couldn't be chance, like Sophie wants to believe?'

'I accept it's not all chance,' Sophie tried to reassure them, and went out to the stables. Bob looked after her fondly.

'Some of it could be pure unconnected spite, perhaps against the stables, and the rest chance, but I don't think so,' Luke said. 'Do you know anything about her family? Did you know her grandmother, and was she well liked in the area?'

Bob shook his head. 'Only her grandfather. I knew him for a year or so, and he was very popular. Oh, I know she's Peter Stein's daughter, and could be considered wealthy already from what she's inherited from her grandfather and her mother and stepfather, and now the money from this London flat. I don't know what her own father left her. She doesn't behave as though she's rich, no expensive clothes or cars, and even Smoke, her new mare, isn't top of the range, just a good medium mount. I suspect,' he added slowly, 'she doesn't want to seem better off than Pru. You know about her, of course?'

'Not a great deal. Tell me.'

'It's only what I've picked up from the villagers, mind. She was the daughter of one of the farm labourers, and had a couple of brothers, much older than she was. I think she was rather spoilt, being the only girl and born when her parents were in their forties. The boys had to help in the garden, and round the farm, from when they were tiny, but there was cash for Pru to have riding clothes and a few lessons, and she had all the time she wanted to work up at the stables, earning rides. Then, when she was sixteen, she up and married a widower who'd retired to the village a year before. Caused quite a stir, that did, he was all of fifty years older than she was. Her father died the following year, people said it was from shame at having a son-in-law older than he was, and her mother moved to live with one of the boys, who'd done well and got a small shop over in Reading. The other's a social worker in Oxford. He's sweet on Sophie but she's not interested in any men, it seems.'

'What happened to Pru's husband?'

'The fellow died rather suddenly. I gather there were all sorts of scurrilous jokes about energetic young wives, but it seemed he'd a bad heart. He left her the house and a big insurance policy and several thousands besides, and though he had a daughter older than Pru, the will didn't mention her, and she didn't get a thing. Pru, of course, moved into Crispins and the girls became partners. They'd always been friends, I believe, and Sophie certainly couldn't have managed the place on her own.'

Luke nodded. 'Thanks. It helps to have the background. I'll drop in again tomorrow.'

'Meanwhile, trust me to keep my eyes open.'

Sophie dithered between the peacock blue shirt and one in a soft yellow. Eventually she chose the yellow, because then she felt the gold chain was not too much. Pru had found an excuse to be out in the stables when Luke arrived, and hadn't returned by the time he'd showered and changed. She appeared to wave them goodbye, and Sophie leaned back in the passenger seat with a sigh of contentment.

'Where are we going?'

'Not far. An Italian place in Wendover. A friend of mine recommended it.'

Luke drove through the winding, confusing lanes without a single hesitation.

'You seem to know the way,' Sophie

commented a little stiffly, conscious that they had barely spoken since setting out, and were almost into the little market town.

Luke grinned. 'I drove this way this morning, to be sure. There's nothing so embarrassing as taking your new girl to a place and losing the way, having to admit to incompetence.'

Sophie laughed, but wondered at the 'new girl'. Did he regard her in that light? And did she mind? How did she regard him? She was so terribly confused, veering between longing for his kisses and distrust of his motives.

They walked a short distance from the car park to a small, outwardly undistinguished restaurant which had once been part of a pub. But inside all was luxury and efficient service. When they had ordered, Sophie turned to Luke. 'You promised your life history today,' she said as lightly as she could, trying to conceal her eagerness to find out about him. 'Your name's French, for a start.'

'My father was French Canadian, but he settled in England when he met my mother, who came from the Midlands. We moved to Paris when I was a child.

They went back to Canada a few years ago, and live there now with my two younger sisters. I went to school here, and Oxford, and decided to base myself here when I began to earn a living in journalism. It's more convenient for the places I go to, and the people I want to write about.'

'Retired politicians.'

'At the moment. There are quite a few of them since the last election. After this series is finished, and my book on Vietnam, I plan a series on European Parliament figures, and the Eurocrats of Brussels and Strasburg. Both lovely cities, and I shall base myself there for a few months.'

Sophie blinked. Somehow she hadn't thought ahead. There hadn't been a great deal of time. She'd had so many other things to worry about, and she hadn't even become accustomed to the idea that Luke might want to keep in touch, but the thought of losing him soon struck her with devastating force. 'When?' she asked. 'I mean, when are you likely to be going there?'

'By the end of the year if all's well.'

They talked of places they'd both been to, and Luke entertained her with stories of his travel journalism, the different way he was sometimes treated when hoteliers knew he was doing a feature on their hotels and facilities, and when he was just an ordinary guest.

Sophie sighed enviously. 'After horses, the thing I'd most like to do is to travel. I once dreamed of being in an international show-jumping team, and going all over the world, but I'm not good enough.'

'You wouldn't see much of the places that way,' Luke said. 'You'd have been too busy, looking after the horses and competing, then out again the minute your competition is over. And one stadium or arena is very like another, only the language and perhaps the ads are different.'

By the time they had coffee Sophie was feeling quite at ease. It had been a wonderful meal, but she couldn't have said what she'd eaten. They walked back to the car park with arms linked, and when, beside the car, Luke turned her towards him and pulled her close she went eagerly.

'Do you trust me?' he asked quietly.

She nodded and lifted her face in mute invitation. Luke's arms tightened round her and he bent his head to hers, their lips meeting with a fierce hunger that made them oblivious to their surroundings. Sophie gave a deep, contented sigh, and as Luke's kiss grew warmer, she strained against him, her arms creeping round his neck, her fingers tangling with his hair, long and springy.

'You are irresistible,' he murmured, 'and I want to eat you!'

Several loud wolf whistles made Sophie leap away from him in alarm, but Luke laughed softly, glancing at half a dozen youths who had come into the car park and were eyeing them with amusement.

'They're jealous I've got the loveliest girl in Buckinghamshire tonight,' he murmured in Sophie's ear, as she buried her face in his shirt in embarrassment. 'But perhaps this isn't the best place to show you how I feel.'

He opened the passenger door, helped her in, and went to his own side. For a while they were followed by the youths on motorcycles, and Sophie felt a sudden spasm of fear. Was the nightmare to begin all over again? Luke, however, soon lost them by turning off the main road, and Sophie realised they hadn't been intending to follow far.

'I expect they were hoping we'd provide further entertainment,' Luke said with a chuckle. Sophie cringed. She'd had to fight off a few amorous youths in the past who'd considered cars ideal places for seduction, and she desperately hoped Luke would not prove to be the same. Her fears were groundless, and he didn't stop until they swept into the drive of Crispins. Only a small porch light was on. 'Pru seems to have gone to bed,' Luke said, his voice trembling with laughter. 'How tactful of her.'

Inside the house, though, he did no more than kiss Sophie lightly on the tip of her nose.

'Off to bed, temptress,' he said briskly. 'I've more work to do tomorrow, and you have to be up early as well. Didn't Pru say there was a gymkhana to prepare for?'

Sophie groaned. 'I'd forgotten. It's midnight now, and I'll have to be up at six. Thank you, Luke, for a lovely evening,' she added shyly.

'We must do it again,' he said, and left Sophie wondering whether he was referring to the meal. That had been wonderful, but she'd never before wanted to kiss anyone, apart from in a spirit of adolescent experimentation, and she'd soon tired of that. Luke's kisses were different, she mused as she prepared for bed. Then her prosaic side reminded the dreamy one that he was much older than the boys she'd known before, and had doubtless had many girlfriends, even lovers. The thought made her shiver. She knew that compared with most of her contemporaries she was inexperienced. She'd heard lots of stories from other girls, of course, and read all the right books, but she'd never been to bed with anyone, never been tempted. If Luke had asked her, though, she'd have gone willingly, eager to know him better, explore his body, and have those warm, tender lips and sensitive hands tease hers into rapturous response.

★ ★ ★ ★

Luke had gone well before Sophie came in from the stables the following morning. He'd said he wanted to take some photographs, and being Sunday, the places he wanted would be quiet.

'Had just a cup of coffee,' Mrs Miller said disapprovingly. 'That's no way to be set up for the day,' she complained. Mrs

Miller, short and rotund, was of the bacon and eggs and sausages, with mushrooms or tomatoes as well as fried bread for breakfast school. She came every morning and never gave up trying to provide it. And then toast and marmalade, with lashings of butter. 'It was what my father ate every day, bless his soul, and he lived to ninety,' she'd explain whenever someone refused her proffered bounty. She was a widow, and had no one else to care for, she explained with monotonous regularity. Pru and Sophie usually took care to have had their own more modest breakfasts before she arrived. The main meal she prepared was substantial enough, and they sometimes had difficulty in managing that.

When he returned that evening Luke had a briefcase full of notes and books he'd bought from Blackwells. 'Sunday opening has its advantages,' he said.

'Travel books?' Pru asked when he'd unloaded them onto the end of the kitchen table.

'I have to keep in touch with what's being published,' he explained. 'Besides, they give me ideas of where I might go myself, to write articles.'

'Aren't you afraid of copying what

they've done?' Pru asked.

'Anyone writing a book will have been there at least two years ago, and there's always something new, a different angle,' he explained.

'How much more work do you have to do? And how can you research travel in a library?'

'I'm reading up background of the countries, sometimes local magazines, but most of what I'm doing now is reading recent papers relating to the politicians I'm interviewing. A couple more days should be enough.'

Pru raised her eyebrows. 'I thought you just went there and described it, or interviewed them and reported what they said.'

'You can do that for some things and places. I try to do wider topics.'

★ ★ ★ ★

The following day, after the excitement of the gymkhana, felt flat. Luke had left early again, and in the afternoon Sophie decided to exercise Faustus, one of the livery horses who hadn't been ridden for several days. He was a powerful hunter, capable of clearing high solid hedges, but a beautifully mannered, mild animal she enjoyed riding as much as she did her own mare. She let him stretch his legs over the paddock jumps first, then set off on a long circuit mainly through woods, but with a few open fields where she could have a clear gallop.

On the last stretch home they were ambling along, horse and rider both pleasantly tired, and Sophie was trying to sort out her feelings towards Luke. He'd made no further attempt to kiss her, or even touch her hand, and she was beginning to think she'd dreamed those earlier kisses and that tender embrace after their meal in Wendover. She was beginning to wonder what she could do to encourage him, for she decided she definitely wanted to do that. Unfortunately every scenario of seduction she'd culled from films or books didn't appeal to her, or made her laugh at the visions conjured up.

She decided she had no imagination, for she hadn't the faintest notion of how to go about it, and gave Faustus the signal to trot on. Without warning a shot whistled past her head, and Faustus leapt sideways, and before Sophie knew what was happening had broken into an uncontrolled gallop. Dimly she heard several shots, but found her hands and mind full as she tried to bring the terrified beast under control.

Thankful that she hadn't been unseated, she clung on, and gradually steadied him so that they entered the stable yard in a slightly more decorous fashion. Faustus was sweating and trembling, though, and Sophie's jeans were covered in foam from his frothing mouth. She slid down from his back as Pru, hearing the commotion of hooves clattering on the cobbles of the yard, ran out of the tack room to investigate.

'What's happened?' she demanded, coming to try and soothe the panting horse.

'On the track above the farm, he suddenly bolted,' Sophie said, shaking herself now the peril was over. 'Some idiot was potting rabbits, I think, too close to the path. The sound of the gun terrified him.'

'Gun?' Pru almost shouted. 'You mean someone's been shooting at you?'

'At me?' Sophie said, and paled as she realised Pru could be right.

'They've tried almost everything else,' Pru said. 'None of the locals would shoot there. Apart from being too near the track, where we ride all the time, there aren't many rabbits there. This time, Sophie, you're going to have to accept it. Someone's trying to kill you, and you can't go on being lucky all the time.'

Chapter Six

They were sitting either side of the kitchen table when Luke returned. Sophie looked pale, and she hadn't changed out of her riding clothes.

'What's happened?' Luke demanded. He wanted to take her in his arms and tell her it would all come right, but something about her rigid attitude prevented him.

'Another attempt,' Pru said curtly.

'It could have been someone shooting rabbits, being careless,' Sophie pleaded.

'She still won't accept the truth,' Pru said, anger roughening her voice. 'Where've you been all day?'

'In the Bodleian,' Luke said, surprised at the aggression in her voice. Then his eyes widened. 'You're not accusing me, are you?'

Pru's gaze held his. 'Why not? Sophie's more ready to accuse me than you. But you had the opportunity for every single event except the first,' she went on furiously, turning back to Luke while Sophie, groaning, put her arms on the table and buried her head in them. 'That could have been a put-up job, to enable you to worm your way into Sophie's confidence, make her trust you. None of the other attacks have succeeded. Maybe they're fakes.'

'What rubbish!' Luke snapped, but Sophie interrupted.

'Pru, you're talking nonsense!'

Pru ignored her. 'You pretended to find that gun after the car chase, frightening Sophie into taking it more seriously, and trusting you. You could have organised, even been part of the kidnap, and been riding that motorbike. Sophie said you were late and seemed flustered meeting her that evening. You could have delivered that beastly parcel, and sent the letter, and you could have tried to push Sophie under the train. We don't know where you were today, you could have shot at Sophie this afternoon.'

'Stop it, Pru!' Sophie almost screamed at her. 'I won't listen to you making these horrible suggestions!'

Luke was listening impassively. 'I grant the possibility,' he said evenly, 'but if you had an accomplice you could have been as responsible. And you would gain if Sophie died. What possible gain do I have?'

'If you married her you'd have her as well as her money.'

'Are you afraid of that happening, Pru?'

Sophie jerked upright and stared at him, her eyes wide.

Pru almost spluttered with fury. 'You arrogant sod! So that's it? Maybe they weren't serious attempts, you just wanted to make Sophie frightened so that you could work on her emotions and sweep her off her feet! Well, you won't if I have anything to say about it!'

Sophie stood up suddenly. 'Shut up, both of you! I'm sick of hearing you throwing insults! It's my life that's threatened, and when it's my marriage neither of you will make or prevent me from doing exactly what I like! You don't own me, either of you! But you've convinced me that someone's out to kill me, and I don't care who it is, I just want it stopped!'

She marched across to the phone, all her former reluctance gone.

'Who are you phoning?' Pru asked.

'Is that the police? This is Sophie Stone, of Crispins Stables. Is Detective Sergeant Pickford available, please?' Sophie said into the phone, staring challengingly over it at the others. 'Never mind. I want to speak to someone about an attempt to murder me. Probably several attempts. Yes, I'll be here. Thanks.'

She put down the receiver.

'Are they coming round?' Pru asked. 'Good. That's about the first sensible thing you've done since the whole business started.'

Sophie stared at her, unsmiling. 'Is it? Well, let's be sensible now and eat that dinner Mrs Miller cooked before the police arrive. It's in the oven. Pru, lay the table please, and Luke, I think we could all do with some wine. There's a bottle in the fridge, and glasses in the end cupboard.'

Luke suppressed a grin. Pru looked as though one of the horses had begun to talk and give her instructions. Sophie ignored them both. She didn't often fling orders around, Pru did most of the organising of the work of the stables, and Sophie normally went along with it because she respected the older girl's experience and

140

competence. But she wasn't going to let anyone boss her around any more.

Luke fetched wine and glasses while Sophie took the casserole and rice from the oven. Pru plonked cutlery down in the middle of the table and looked as though she was about to refuse to sit down, but Sophie gave her a friendly smile, inclined her head towards the chair, and the older girl eventually sat down and began to serve out the meal.

They had just finished when a police car drew up outside. Two uniformed constables came in and took notes, asked a few questions, and then went off to look at the track Sophie had been riding on and ask questions round the village.

'We'll pass it on to Detective Sergeant Pickford,' one of them said as they left. 'He'll no doubt be out to see you tomorrow. Meanwhile, take care, and let us know if anything else happens.'

'Like if they finally succeed in killing you,' Pru said in disgust.

Sophie slumped in her chair. 'I'm exhausted. I'm off to bed.'

She went out of the room without a backward glance. Pru turned to Luke, once more aggressive.

141

'Do you mean to stay here any longer?' she asked.

Luke nodded. 'Until Sophie asks me to leave,' he replied quietly. Pru snorted in disgust, and began piling the dinner plates into a bowl of soapy water as he left the room.

★ ★ ★ ★

Sophie was relieved when Pru appeared the following morning and immediately apologised for her bad temper. 'I'm just so worried for you,' she said.

'I'm worried too,' Sophie confessed. 'And I want Luke to stay here. I trust him.'

'OK, I'll keep mum.'

She apologised to Luke too, and while her attitude could not be described as affable, it was at least neutral. Luke, saying he'd finished at the Bodleian for now, was in old jeans and a tee shirt, and insisted on helping with the early chores. When Detective Sergeant Pickford arrived and had talked to them, they all walked to where Sophie had been shot at.

'The men found some spent cartridges behind the hedge,' Pickford informed them.

'They're being examined now, they seem new, but are a common sort and we don't hold out much hope they'll tell us anything.'

They turned to walk back. 'It was fortunate the horse wasn't hit, and bolted,' Pickford said. 'We know about the kidnap attempt here, but what about these incidents in London? Have you recalled any more about those? You have no witnesses, I suppose?'

Sophie shook her head, then paused. 'I haven't a clue about the two men who saved me from being pushed under the train, but when the motorbike nearly ran me down I spoke to an elderly man. I offered him a lift in my taxi, but he said he lived just across the road. I think I'd recognise him again. And there's just a chance he might know the jogger. But he didn't see any more than I did, we neither of us saw the number plate.'

'I'll take a description of this man, and the local police can follow it up. Is there anything else you can remember, however small and insignificant it might seem?'

'There was the man who seemed to be watching the flat,' Sophie said slowly.

'What?'

'What man?' Luke demanded.

Sophie explained. 'It seemed as though I was imagining things afterwards. But I did have quite a good look at him, and the boy delivering newspapers spoke to him. He might know who he was.'

★ ★ ★ ★

For more than a week Sophie waited for the next disaster to strike. When nothing happened she began to relax, the strained expression left her eyes, and she chafed at the limitations on her movements that both Pru and Luke insisted on.

They seemed to have agreed a truce. It was wary, probably fragile, but Sophie was grateful to them. For the moment she could forget their mutual, suppressed antagonism. She had enough to think about, and could hardly bear the tension between her fear of whoever it was stalking her with murderous intent, and a different kind of trepidation that Luke's feelings towards her seemed to have cooled.

He'd made no further attempt to kiss, or even touch her. She began to think he'd regretted those earlier embraces. His remark about marrying her had, she concluded after deep and serious analysis of every word and nuance of expression, been simply an example in his argument with Pru, not in any way intended as expressing some intention, vague or positive. He'd been joking, that time in London, when she'd been so angry and flung the accusation at him that it was his objective.

After a few days Sophie persuaded Luke that he didn't need to hover round her all the time. She promised faithfully never to leave the house or the stable yard, where it would be far more difficult to attack her. Others could do the work in the paddocks and accompany rides, or exercise the livery horses. No one else seemed to be at risk. Luke, however, was determined to stay around, and she wanted him there, but he needed more clothes and some notes from his flat, so one day he agreed to leave her while he went to collect them.

'You could come with me,' he suggested when Pru had vanished to make some phone calls.

Sophie smiled. 'Thanks, but we have another gymkhana tomorrow, and lots of preparations. I'll be safe. And I don't fancy going to London in this heat.'

He was back within three hours, just as the girls were coming from the stable yard into lunch.

'Your car's been damaged,' Sophie said, walking round to inspect a dented rear wing. 'What happened? They're not trying to kill you now, are they?'

'Some idiot trying to park in a space smaller than his car bumped into it while I was in the flat,' Luke said. 'It's not bad, I expect it can be hammered out.'

'It's the nearside,' Pru pointed out, sounded accusing.

'Pru, in London there are lots of one-way streets,' Sophie said. 'People park where they can.'

'You must have broken several speed limits to get there and back so quickly,' Pru said, not quite managing to keep the disapproval out of her voice.

'Yes,' he said shortly. 'But I managed to phone the police. They've traced your old man in Holland Park Avenue,' he went on, turning to Sophie, 'and the jogger, but they couldn't add to what you'd said. The man watching the flat they can't trace, the newspaper boy didn't know him, said the chap had just asked him the time.'

'Thanks,' Sophie smiled at him. 'I didn't

think they'd know anything more.'

★ ★ ★ ★

On the following day Luke settled down to work on a table in his bedroom. It would be more convenient, Sophie said, than to work in the kitchen, since he could leave his papers out. He'd only managed to sort out the notes he'd fetched from home, putting them in their correct folders, before Mrs Miller called him down for coffee. It was early, since the girls were just about to set off for the gymkhana. He was still thinking about his work, and taking little notice of anything else beyond giving Sophie an abstracted smile.

She was frowning over a postcard. 'That's odd.'

'What is?' Pru asked, coming into the kitchen.

'This card,' Sophie said, holding it out to her. 'It's from Gerard, saying he's on his way to visit me. But he says Wednesday, which was yesterday. He never arrived.'

'Gerard? Your half-brother?' Luke asked, suddenly alert and quite forgetting his own work.

'Yes. He's supposed to be with the

family in Australia.'

'How old is he?'

'Seventeen and a half.'

'Were you told specifically that he was in Australia?'

Sophie tried to recall the telephone conversation. 'I phoned their house and there was no reply, so I phoned the office where Franz works. They told me there that he was on holiday. I'm sure they said with his family.'

'It's highly likely a seventeen-year-old would prefer an independent holiday to one with his parents,' Luke said thoughtfully.

'He wants to study English at university, doesn't he?' Pru put in. 'He came over for a few weeks last summer to improve his English.'

'Could he have meant next week?' Luke took the card Sophie was holding and looked at it. 'No, he has the date right.'

Sophie sighed and sat down, pouring out more coffee. 'Where is he?'

'Boys that age aren't terribly reliable,' Pru said. 'He may have decided to stay longer with some other friends, or met some girl.'

'He could have phoned.'

They could do nothing, however, but

Sophie looked worried for the rest of the day, even while winning more rosettes at the gymkhana. The following morning she had dark circles round her eyes, and refused all Mrs Miller's offers of breakfast, saying she couldn't eat anything, just wanted coffee, strong and black.

Mrs Miller shrugged and departed to clean the bathroom, muttering dire warnings about anorexia and caffeine poisoning. When she was out of earshot Pru leaned forward urgently.

'Sophie, could Gerard be behind the attacks on you? We don't know how long he's been in this country, and he can drive, can't he?'

Sophie stared at her in amazement. 'It wasn't Gerard in the Volvo, and I don't see where he could have got hold of two guns, even if he does want to murder me! Oh, I'm so tired of all this!'

She stormed out of the kitchen, and after a moment Luke followed. He eventually found her in the barn where they stored hay, leaning against a stack of bales and desperately trying to hold back her tears. When he pulled her to him she at first resisted, but then her rigidity left her, and she buried her face in his chest.

'Sophie, sweetheart,' he murmured, cradling her close and stroking her hair. Gradually she recovered her calm, and began to pull away from him. She couldn't afford to give way like this, revealing her need of him, or her fear.

'I'm sorry, Luke, I didn't mean to make an exhibition of myself,' she said, forcing herself to smile. 'I expect there's a very simple explanation why Gerard's not here, but if Pru goes on insinuating it's my brothers behind all this I shall say something unforgivable! I know I will!'

'Come back in and have some toast. Mrs Miller's right, you do need to eat,' he urged, and Sophie, nodding, blew her nose fiercely and threw up her head before marching across to the house and into the kitchen.

Mrs Miller was still upstairs, but she had placed the morning's newspapers on the table. Luke cut bread and put it in the toaster while Sophie picked up the papers to make room for a plate. When Luke turned round she was staring in disbelief at the one she held in her hand.

'Darling, what is it?' he said, and she handed him the paper and pointed wordlessly to a picture on the front page.

He scanned it swiftly.

There was a blurred photograph of a young man, upon which a large question mark had been superimposed. ACCIDENT VICTIM'S FAMILY SOUGHT, the headlines screamed. The item described how a young motorcyclist, riding a German registered bike, and carrying a German passport in the name of Gerard Stein, had been knocked off his bike by another vehicle, believed to be a large blue saloon car, on the steep hill leading down from the M40 junction into the centre of High Wycombe. The accident had happened on Wednesday. Before he lapsed into a coma, the article went on, he had said something to indicate that he was on his way to visit relatives. 'Unfortunately the nurse with him had only a basic understanding of the German language, and before the victim could supply more details, or a German speaker be found, he became unconscious.' The paper went on to appeal for anyone who knew the victim, or had witnessed the accident, to come forward, and then recounted the many other accidents which had occurred through the steepness of Marlow Hill and the speeding of careless drivers.

'He'll be in Wycombe Hospital, it's near the foot of that hill,' Sophie said. 'Tell Pru. I'll be back when I can.'

'Wait.'

'Wait? What for? It's my brother!'

'Stop a minute! I'll take you, but before we go rushing off to Wycombe let's telephone. It's quite possible he's been transferred to a specialist unit at another hospital.'

Sophie sank back onto her chair. 'Sorry. Yes, please will you phone?'

The toast forgotten, Luke managed to get through to the hospital. After a short conversation he put the receiver down and turned to Sophie. 'They've moved him to an Oxford hospital.' He dialled again, while Sophie waited anxiously.

'How is he?' she asked when he'd finished.

'Still in a coma, but no worse. I understand they'll be operating soon, but she wouldn't give me any more details. You can go and see him any time.'

'Try and stop me!' Sophie muttered, standing up. The colour had returned to her cheeks and her eyes were glittering.

'Go and change.'

'What? How can I waste more time?'

'Gerard doesn't know you're coming, and you won't be very popular if you go into a nice clean ward smelling of horses and horse manure.'

For a moment Sophie didn't understand, then she gave a brief nod. She ran for the stairs, and within five minutes came back dressed in a pale green skirt and white shirt, wearing sandals instead of riding boots. She'd washed her face and combed her hair, and even stopped to put on a coat of lip gloss.

'Good girl,' Luke said, and took her hand.

'Pru. I must tell her.'

'I've written her a note. Come on, let's go.'

Forty minutes later he pulled into the hospital car park, lucky to find a space. They hurried into the building and followed the signs to the wards. At the door they spoke to a Sister who smiled reassuringly at Sophie.

'He's stable, and I've seen far worse cases recover completely,' she said in a gentle Irish accent. 'He broke both legs, and they'll set those tomorrow, or in a few days. We don't think there are any serious internal injuries, but he was concussed too, went into a wall, and that's caused the coma. Do you want to see him now or wait until his brother has gone?'

'His brother?' Sophie said. 'Helmut? But how can he be here?'

'I think he said his name was Rob or Rod, not Helmut. He's got a strong American accent, anyway.'

Sophie cast an anguished look at Luke. 'Rod's supposed to be in New York! On a course. How can he be here, and with Gerard? How did he find out about the accident?'

'Do you know how he came to know about this?' Luke asked the Sister.

'I think he said he'd seen it in the local paper,' she said, 'but you can ask him. Come this way now.'

They followed her to a side room, and Sophie looked fearfully at the bed. Gerard was attached to what seemed like dozens of drips and machines. A tall dark man a few years younger than Luke who had been sitting beside the bed looked round and rose to his feet, smiling at Sophie. He looked pale and exhausted, his forehead creased with worry, his eyes bloodshot.

'Sophie! They told me you'd called and were coming in.'

'He looks terrible!' she exclaimed, allowing him to kiss her on the cheek. 'Will he get better?'

'Of course he will! He had a bad knock, but he'll be right as rain in a few days, and his legs will mend. They said the breaks were clean.'

'What are you doing in England, and why didn't you let me know you were here?'

'I only arrived on Monday, the middle of the night, it seemed, for a course taking place at an Oxford college.'

'You didn't tell me you were coming on a course.'

'It was last minute, I took over a place of someone who was sick.'

'Why didn't you call me?'

'I meant to, but I didn't have the energy. I was still getting over an illness, was jet-lagged, and trying to cope with the course. Today someone showed me the local paper, they knew my name was Stein too, and so I came right on over. I was going to come and see you when I knew how badly injured he was. No point in worrying you until I knew that.'

Sophie nodded slowly. After a few minutes the Sister came back and suggested they ought to leave now. 'You can come back any time. But perhaps one of you can tell us how to contact his parents?'

'They're on holiday in Australia,' Sophie said, and Rod looked at her in surprise.

'How did you know that? Had Gerard seen you or called?'

'It doesn't matter. I have his father's office number, they might be able to get in touch,' she went on to the Sister. 'Do you want to do it, or shall I try?'

'If there are any problems we'll be more likely to pull weight,' the Sister said with a chuckle. 'Why don't you go and get a cuppa before you go home? There's a cafeteria.'

They nodded and went back along the corridors. It wasn't until they were seated at a small table by the window, surrounded by waiting patients, visitors, restless toddlers, and several people in wheelchairs, that Luke introduced himself.

'I've read some of your articles,' Rod said. 'Great stuff. How do you come to know my kid sister?'

'We met through a friend,' Sophie said swiftly, kicking Luke's ankle under the table. 'Luke happened to be there when I read the paper and he brought me in. But I think we'd better be getting back now, or Pru will never forgive me for leaving her to do all the dirty work. What's your Oxford number? I'll phone tonight and you must come over and see us before you go back to the States.'

'It's a college number, in a student block, and I don't have it on me. Thing is, I doubt if the main switchboard would be able to find me, or even pass on messages. But I'll call you tomorrow. I'll come and see Gerard again, and perhaps I can take you out for a meal?'

'OK. Now we must go,' she repeated, and stood up, leaving her coffee untasted.

She was silent all the way back to the stables, frowning down at her hands. As they entered the village she suddenly spoke. 'Luke, please can we stop for a minute and talk?'

'What is it?'

'I don't know. It just doesn't add up. He looked dreadful, and as far as I know Rod's never been seriously ill in his life. And if he had been ill surely Arlene would have told me. He didn't even tell us which college he was at. And I very much doubt if the local paper here is read very widely in Oxford at all, let alone the colleges. Luke, I'm beginning to distrust everyone and everything! Am I going mad?'

Chapter Seven

'You're in no fit state to work,' Luke told her. 'We'll go and have a quiet lunch somewhere, and talk.'

Sophie shook her head. 'I couldn't face anyone, not even a waiter or barmaid.'

'A picnic, then? I'll get something from the village shop, and we'll drive to a quiet spot and sit in the car.'

She nodded. 'Thanks. I need an hour or so just to sit still and think.'

'Wait here, I'll only be a few minutes.'

When Luke emerged from the village shop with a plastic bag bulging with food she laughed. 'How long is this picnic going to last? You've got enough there for several days!'

'I didn't know what to buy,' he confessed, slinging the bag on the rear seat and starting the car.

They drove up into the hills, and eventually came to an open, grassy spot high on an escarpment, overlooking the Vale of Aylesbury. For a wonder on a beautiful summer day no one else was in the small parking area, and they had sole use of the entire site.

'Let's go under those trees,' Luke suggested, and handed Sophie a car rug to carry while he seized the plastic bag.

They spread out the rug, and he unpacked the food. Sophie eyed the selection in amazement. 'It looks like you're catering for a party. Crisps, nuts, sausage rolls, and enormous ones, pork pies, fruit pies, cakes, biscuits, and half a dozen canned drinks.'

'I thought of the vitamins too,' he protested with a laugh. 'Apples, oranges, and bananas. And a bottle of wine to cheer us up.'

'I suppose you're the sort of man who carries a knife with gadgets for taking stones out of horses' hooves,' Sophie said, amused. 'Does it have a corkscrew as well?'

For a moment he looked chastened, then grinned disarmingly. 'I don't even have a stone-remover. I could knock the top off with a stone?'

'And then we take turns at drinking from the broken top? Thanks, let's have it tonight! I'll make do with fizzy orange.'

Sophie found she was hungrier than she'd expected. It was partly, she knew, a sense of optimism that Gerard was going to be all right, but also being here with Luke, determined, for an hour at least, to forget the worries that beset her, the attacks which she had come to accept were not accidents, but deliberate murderous attempts. She ate hungrily, drank to wash down the cloying pastry, and then lay down on the rug, nibbling an apple. Luke tidied away the uneaten food and the debris of packaging into the bag and sat looking down at her. She smiled lazily up at him, then her eyes clouded.

'I suppose I ought to be concentrating on problems,' she said reluctantly. 'I'm being an ostrich. Most of the time I've refused to believe they weren't accidents, but I can't ignore it any longer. Do you think Gerard was attacked too?'

'I wondered the same thing. But that hill is very steep, it's an accident black spot, and if he didn't know it he could have misjudged. Especially as he can't have been riding a motorbike for very long, and won't be used to driving on the left side of the road.'

'That's what I try to believe. But it seems one incident too many. And Rod being here makes it even odder.'

'How much did you see of your half-brothers?'

'Mom came back to England before Dad died, before Gerard was born, and I was too young to remember Rod from that time. But when Mom married again she felt we ought to know one another, so until she died they both came to stay with us for part of every summer, and I sometimes stayed with their mothers.'

'So you know one another pretty well?'

'I suppose so. We didn't quarrel much. No doubt if they'd been full brothers, and we lived together, we'd have fought all the while! Tony, Rod's step-father, had two sons a bit older than Rod, and he once said they fought endlessly, and never seemed to have any sort of truce.'

'Why are you suspicious about Rod's being here?'

'He works in a bank, and as he once explained, in tedious detail, the American banking system is quite different from ours in England. What kind of course would an

American banker come to in Oxford?'

'It need not be to do with his job.'

'Recreational, you mean?'

'Perhaps. Or it could be to do with international trade, or some international organisations, or computer systems. You can't be sure.'

'But how could he have been here all along? The girl you spoke to said he had just a week's holiday.'

'But she didn't know him personally.'

'And you didn't ask him. We'll be able to ask more details tomorrow. I expect we'll see him at the hospital.'

'We?' Sophie asked softly. Luke was helping her so much, even though he'd made no attempt even to touch her during this picnic, when they had solitude, a grassy bed, and were sleepy and replete after all the food. Most other boys and men she'd ever known would have seized the opportunity for kissing and tried for even more. She didn't know whether to be glad or sorry. Much as she'd enjoyed his fleeting embraces, she decided now wasn't the time or place, and he had the sensitivity to recognise that. If he wanted to kiss her again, she thought rather bleakly. Perhaps he didn't. Maybe he regretted what little had happened so far. Perhaps she'd read too much into what, for him, had been no more than a casual embrace, like social kissing.

She was silent as they drove back to Crispins, and brusque with Pru when the older girl demanded to know where they'd been all this time.

'I rang the hospital when you didn't come back for lunch. I thought something dreadful had happened to Gerard. They said you only stayed a few minutes. I've been so worried.'

'You needn't have been. You knew Luke was with me.'

Pru opened her mouth and then snapped it closed. 'How was Gerard?' she asked after a pause.

While Luke disappeared to resume his interrupted work, Sophie explained. 'They say he'll be OK, but he's still in a coma, and surely they can't know for certain whether he'll come out of that?'

'You must spend as much time with him as you need to,' Pru said. 'We'll manage here.'

'I don't feel I'm pulling my weight.' Sophie was remorseful. Pru was on edge, but she'd had to cope with more than usual for the past few weeks, and perhaps it wasn't surprising. Also, could she be jealous? Her boyfriend, the man she'd met on her skiing holiday, was in some distant country, and she didn't know when she'd see him again. Even if Luke's attentions to herself were not as serious as Pru thought, she could be missing Guy and resentful of Luke's presence. 'I'll go and change right away. And I won't have to spend long at the hospital. There isn't much point until Gerard's out of his coma.'

★ ★ ★ ★

Three days later, as Sophie was entering the hospital, passing the cafeteria, she saw a tall, blonde woman tapping on the glass partition between it and the corridor. She and Luke walked round to join her. 'Karen? You got here! Oh, thank goodness, I thought they might not be able to contact you!'

'My dear!' Karen hugged her closely. 'We've just been to see him. There's no change, but they insist he'll be all right.'

Sophie turned to Luke. 'This is Gerard's mother, Frau Hoffman, and her husband, Franz.'

Luke had insisted on going to the hospital with her even when she protested that she was capable of driving into Oxford herself, and was taking him away from his work for far too long. Now he drew two chairs across and Sophie introduced them.

'Where are Helmut and Trudi?' she asked.

'We sent them to my mother in Frankfurt,' Franz said in perfect English. 'We were on a friend's yacht, but fortunately he had radio and the police were able to contact us when my secretary telephoned. We got a flight back to Frankfurt at once, and left them there when we came on to London. There was no point in making them come here.'

'Where are you staying? Have you found a hotel yet?'

'No, we hired a car at Heathrow and drove straight here. We passed a hotel at the autobahn—the motorway exit. We can try there.'

'Come and stay with me,' Sophie said impulsively. 'I've still one spare bedroom, Grandfather's house is huge. It will be better than waiting in an hotel.'

'We couldn't put you to so much trouble, dear,' Karen began, but Sophie shook her head.

'It's no trouble. It would be miserable in an hotel, and as I know you like riding, Franz, you can help exercise the horses for me. I've left everything to Pru recently, or so it feels, and you'd be doing me a favour.'

'And if you insist I will do some of the cooking,' Karen declared.

'If Mrs Miller will let you,' Sophie said, smiling. 'Do you want to go now? You must be exhausted after that flight. I can draw you a map to find the way. Or will you wait until we've been to see Gerard and follow us? We won't be long. Poor Gerard, there isn't much point when he doesn't know we're there.'

'They said he was conscious for a few minutes early this morning,' Karen said, wiping a tear from her eye. 'He's getting better, and they plan to operate tomorrow. His poor legs!'

Franz put his arm round her shoulders. 'Don't cry, *liebling*. He'll be as good as new soon, and when they'll let him travel we'll take him straight back home.' He pulled out a large scale map. 'Show me where your house is, Sophie, and we'll go straight there.'

Sophie and Luke left them then, and went to see Gerard. The Sister smiled at them as they went in.

'He's having plenty of visitors,' she remarked brightly. 'His brother came yesterday, and today his cousins, and his parents, now you.'

'What cousins?' Sophie asked, curious. 'As far as I know he hasn't got any.' She knew that both Karen and Franz were only children.

'A young couple. I think they said they were his cousins. They were in their mid-twenties, I guess, though the girl might have been younger.'

'What's wrong?' Luke asked quietly as they stood looking down at Gerard.

'I don't think he has any cousins. She may have been mistaken, but who apart from his family knows he's here, or would want to visit? Could it have been the press? Do you think they've realised he's Peter's son?'

'Shall we ask the staff not to allow anyone else in?' Luke suggested.

'I don't see how we can. That's up to them and his parents.'

'It might be wise to tell them he has no cousins, in case it is reporters and they try again.'

Sophie shook her head. 'I suppose they could have been friends. After all, we don't know who he's been with since he's been in England. Karen might know who they were.'

They left soon afterwards and drove straight back to the stables. The Hoffmanns had arrived and Mrs Miller was fussing around them, trying to insist that they took naps in the big spare room that had once been Sophie's grandfather's. Exhausted though they looked they were refusing, saying they would go to bed early, but if they slept now would be awake all night. After lunch, though, they both stretched out on loungers beside the swimming pool and slept.

Sophie was teaching some pupils in the jumping paddock when Pru, back from an accompanied ride, hailed her. 'I need to go into Aylesbury,' she said apologetically. 'Can you cope for a couple of hours if I go now?'

'Of course I can. If I need another pair of hands Luke will help.'

'I don't know how the poor man is

getting any of his work done,' Pru said, frowning. 'Perhaps he'll go home now the Hoffmanns are here. After all, they're family of a sort, aren't they?'

Sophie was feeling guilty too. She knew that Luke was sitting up late over his book, since she'd twice seen the light on in the room he was using when she'd been lying sleepless well after midnight. She didn't want him to go. It might be selfish of her, but she felt safer when he was near. And she was restless, wondering if his care for her meant more than simple friendship.

There was no hospital visiting the following day, when Gerard was due for his operation, and Sophie tried to keep her mind off it by doing all the most unpleasant chores which she always left as long as possible. The operation had been set for mid-afternoon, and they didn't expect to hear before dinnertime. Karen was hoping to be able to go and see her son, if only for a few minutes, later that evening. They were drinking coffee out by the pool, despite the gathering darkness, since the weather was still exceptionally hot for September, when there was a ring at the front door.

'I'll get it,' Pru said, and went through the house. She was away for several minutes, and when she came back she was walking slowly, her hand covering her mouth, followed by a tall, thin man wearing an old tweed jacket and, incongruously, a tartan bow tie.

He glanced round swiftly, then went to Karen. 'Frau Hoffmann?'

'Yes. What is it? Who are you?'

He pulled one of the chairs to sit beside her and took her hands in his. 'I'm the surgeon who operated on your son's broken legs this afternoon. I'm sorry, Frau Hoffmann, but I'm afraid he died while under the anaesthetic.'

Pru, competent as ever, called their own doctor who sedated Karen, and then helped to put the distraught mother to bed. Franz was sitting with her while Pru, Luke and Sophie huddled round the empty fireplace in the drawing room.

'I don't believe it,' Sophie kept saying. 'There must have been something wrong that the doctors didn't know about. The coma, perhaps they should have waited, not operated until he was stronger.'

'The surgeon said there would be a post-mortem,' Luke said. 'They'll discover then what went wrong.'

'It won't bring him back,' she said bleakly.

'No, but if there was something wrong, which we didn't know about—irreparable brain damage, for example—it might help to know.'

'When will they do it?' Pru asked quietly.

'Tomorrow, I think he said. We'll know by tomorrow evening.'

Pru sighed. 'Lord, I'm tired. I must go to bed. Will you be OK, Sophie?'

'Yes, but I can't go to bed, I'd never sleep.'

'I should have got some sleeping tablets for you too.'

Sophie shuddered. 'No thanks. But I feel like finishing up the bottle of whisky.'

'Sit quietly for a while. I'll stay with you,' Luke suggested, and with a sardonic look at him Pru raised her eyebrows and left the room.

Sophie was sitting on the hearthrug, her arms round her knees as she curled into a small ball. She stared intently down at her knees, and jumped slightly when Luke touched her shoulder.

'Come and curl up on the sofa,' he said, half-lifting her to her feet. She went, unresisting, and let him pull her into his arms, burying her face into his chest and breathing deeply as he gently stroked her hair and back.

She was trying to recall every single thing that had happened during the past few days. Suddenly she sat up. 'How will we tell Rod?' she asked. 'I haven't seen him again, and he didn't phone, though he said he would. We don't know where he is, which college his course is at, where he's staying, or even when his course finishes. Luke, he might be ill again, in hospital himself.'

'You'll hear if he is, but there's nothing we can do now. He may have left the number with the hospital, but in any case he'll probably telephone to ask how the operation went.'

Sophie sniffed. 'Poor Rod, hearing it like that, and being all alone. I'm so lucky to have you—I mean, to have your company. Pru too. Do you think it would be possible, in the morning, to telephone all the colleges and try to trace him?'

'There wouldn't be much point. We don't know what course he's on, they'd have to search endless lists of names. He'll get in touch with you when he hears.'

'I suppose so.'

They sat without speaking for some time, and gradually Sophie's eyes closed. Luke contemplated carrying her up to bed, but decided he'd risk waking her. He managed to arrange a couple of cushions at one end of the sofa and lower Sophie onto them without rousing her. Then he went to fetch her duvet and tucked it round her. She might not be very comfortable, but she would sleep for a while.

He went to his own bed, and woke in the morning to find there had been a heavy storm during the night. The rain was still pelting down relentlessly. He'd left his window open and the curtains were flapping wetly against the glass. As he leant out to draw the window closed he saw Sophie, in her jeans and an anorak, trudging across to the stables. Hastily he pulled on his own jeans and a thin sweater and ran downstairs. It was still early and no one else was around, but the kitchen door had been unlocked and he followed Sophie across the yard.

She was in Smoke's loose box, brushing the mare down with fierce, relentless strokes. She glanced up as Luke halted outside.

'Surely it's too wet to ride,' he said gently.

'Yes. But I have to do something!'

'Let me help you.' He took another curry comb and set to, working at the mare's other flank.

'Nothing's gone right since I met you,' Sophie said suddenly, and Luke, startled, dropped the comb. As he bent to pick it up Smoke jerked restlessly and he had to move swiftly out of the way of her feet.

'What do you mean? Not that I'm the cause of all these disasters, I hope?'

'Of course not. I was just thinking that we've never known one another in ordinary, normal, peaceful circumstances. It's difficult to know what a person's like when such crazy things keep happening, one after the other and no chance, almost, to take a breath in between.'

'If they hadn't happened we might never have met,' he said briskly. 'And that, Sophie, would have been a terrible loss for me.'

She stood still, holding Smoke's pale grey mane up against her cheek, and stared across the mare's withers at him. Her green eyes were huge, their size emphasised by the dark circles beneath, and her dark cap of hair contrasted with her pale face. In the gloom of the stable it was all black and white and grey, apart from the vivid green of her eyes, and the rain pounding down on the roof added to the air of melancholy.

Then she bent her head and began brushing Smoke's shoulder. Ten minutes later, when Luke suggested they ought to go back into the house and find something to eat she nodded, put away the brushes, and walked out of the stable in front of him.

The rain beat down all day. The surgeon had promised to come over with the post-mortem findings as soon as he had them. He too, he'd pointed out gently, had an interest in them. He was confident everything relating to the operation had been normal, and he wanted to know what had caused Gerard's death. Towards the end of a dinner which no one had been able to eat, when they were staring at the large bowl of gooseberry crumble Mrs Miller had left for them, they heard a car pulling up outside.

Karen was at the door before the visitor had reached it. She almost dragged him into the drawing room, and the others crowded in after them.

'Well?' she demanded.

'Not well, I'm afraid,' he said heavily. 'Please sit down, Frau Hoffman.'

'Has the cause of my step-son's death been established?' Franz asked.

'It hasn't been established exclusively yet, more tests have to be done, but he had a massive blood clot. There are indications that air was injected into your son's veins.'

'What?' Pru interrupted. 'You mean he was murdered? I can't believe that could be possible!'

'We don't yet know for certain whether it was or how it was injected, if it was that,' the surgeon replied. 'Air bubbles in the bloodstream can have fatal consequences.'

'That's preposterous!' Franz almost shouted. 'How can such a criminal thing be allowed? Have the police been called?'

'I agree it's tragic, but we don't yet know how it happened. It may be faulty equipment, human error, a number of possibilities, we simply don't know. An enquiry is being mounted at once, naturally, and you will be kept fully informed.'

'I should hope so! I want my own

doctors to be involved in any investigation, too!'

'If you wish. I understand your concern, and believe me, mine is as great. I need to know how such an unnecessary death came about, and there will be no cover-up if any blame can be proven. If you can tell me who to contact I will make the arrangements immediately.'

After he left there was a stunned silence. Karen was huddled into an armchair, and her husband sat on the arm, holding her close. Pru rose and beckoned to Sophie and Luke. They slipped from the room and into the kitchen.

'Sophie, where's Rod?'

'We haven't heard from him. Why? I'm starting to get worried about him, too.'

'Don't you see? Someone killed Gerard, they've been trying to kill you, and the only reason is that they want your money from your father's books.'

Luke stared at her. 'Can you explain? I imagine the royalties and film payments on Peter Stein's books are large. What are the conditions that go with them? Who has the money?'

Sophie explained, her voice expressionless. 'Each of his wives, on divorce, had a cash settlement. He was already rich before his books began to make another fortune. He settled the royalties from each of his books on us children. The first four went to Rod, before I was born. Then four to me, and it so happened Gerard got the book that was published while Karen was expecting him, and the two published posthumously. Two of mine were the biggest earners, with films and lots of foreign editions, so I have a much larger amount than the boys. The money is in trust until we each become twenty-five, so Rod had his this year.'

'And if one of you dies? Did he make provision for that? Does your share go to your mothers?'

'No, if one of us dies before the age of twenty-five it's to be split equally between the survivors. After that age we can leave it how we choose.'

Luke banged the table with his fist. 'What a preposterous scheme! It's an incitement to murder!'

'For Rod,' Pru said calmly.

'No!' Sophie said, distressed. 'I just don't believe Rod would do that! He's not a murderer!'

'We don't know where he's been the last

few weeks while you've been suffering these attacks. We think he was at work, but he was in England a few days ago.'

'That could be explained, he was on a course,' Sophie said.

'Perhaps, and for your sake I hope so. But he seems to have disappeared now, which is suspicious. He visited Gerard just before the operation. He could have injected air into him. You've had some remarkably lucky escapes, but it's better not to depend entirely on luck. I think you should go into hiding somewhere.'

'Run away?'

'If you like. Go somewhere right away from here, find a quiet hotel, and stay put for a week or two. Perhaps, if they discover what happened to Gerard, the police will arrest someone, and then you'll be able to come back, safely.'

'But the stables,' Sophie asked. 'How would you manage without me?'

'I can cope. The school holidays are over, we won't be so busy, and if necessary I'll employ another groom.'

'I don't want to leave you here. You could be in danger, it could be someone attacking the business, and Gerard—well, Mr Williamson could be wrong. It might just be some awful coincidence.'

'Pru's right, you ought to get away,' Luke said slowly. 'But I've a better idea. An hotel wouldn't be very pleasant, but I have a cottage in Cornwall. Usually I rent it out for the summer, but my tenants left at the end of August. It's empty. I could take you there until it's all over, and no one would know where we've gone.'

Chapter Eight

'Sophie's not going away to some remote place with you!' Pru declared impetuously.

Luke raised his eyebrows. 'You've made your distrust of me quite clear, Pru, but this is for Sophie to decide.'

Pru hesitated. 'I don't trust anyone,' she muttered after a while. 'I think Sophie would be better off away from everyone.'

'Except you.'

'That's preposterous! Now you're accusing me of trying to kill her? How could I, even if it made sense? I wasn't in that car, or in London!'

'Presumably you'd want to know where

she was, or are you proposing she goes to ground and none of us will ever know if anything happens to her?' Luke asked, ignoring Pru's furious outburst.

'Of course she can't be totally isolated, but if everyone knows where she is, it defeats the objective. One person should know, and I think, as her partner and lifelong friend, I have that right!'

'Stop it, both of you!' Sophie marched across the room and stood looking out of the window, her back rigid with tension. Dare she trust Luke? She wanted to, so desperately. Then Sophie sighed and turned round. She had to trust someone. 'It's me they're trying to kill, whoever they are, and I'll decide what to do, and what chances to take. Do you mean it, Luke?'

'I can work just as well there as here—better probably. And I'd meant to go there soon just to check it out, before the end of the summer.'

'Sophie,' Pru said urgently, 'it's foolish to trust anyone. Luke, I'm not accusing you, but it's true we don't know you, and apart from the first incident you could have done all of them. You could even have swiped Gerard off his bike.'

Luke gave a sharp crack of laughter.

'Your imagination's out of control, Pru! How could I have even known about his being in England, let alone that he'd be there on that hill at a particular time? Sophie didn't even know he was in England until his postcard came the following day! And it's one of the least efficient ways of deliberately murdering someone that I've ever heard.'

'I don't know. You could have people all over the place, watching. You would have needed someone else for the original chase. And don't forget, your car's damaged, it happened that same day when you said you'd been to London, and it's the near back wing, which would have been how his bike was hit. And you went to see him just before the operation.'

'With a syringe full of air sticking out of my jeans pocket?'

'I don't know how you managed it. You could have found one on the ward somewhere.'

'I doubt if they leave many scattered around,' Luke said contemptuously. 'This is wild speculation, based on nothing at all except that you don't like me.'

'And we were together when we went to see Gerard,' Sophie said. 'You might as well accuse me, or think we did it together!'

Pru held her head in her hands. 'I don't know what to think! But I know I'd go crazy with worry if I didn't know where you were.'

'I'll telephone every day,' Sophie said gently.

'I'd rather know where you were. How about if I wanted to get in touch with you? If something happened and you couldn't phone?'

'You can have the phone number,' Luke said briskly. 'But we ought to be going soon. I suggest we slip away very early, say four in the morning, before it's light. We'll use my car, and if anyone's watching the house they're unlikely to be there so early in the morning.'

'Shall we tell Karen?'

Pru shook her head. 'She's too upset now. I'll tell her tomorrow, that you're afraid and have gone away. Don't worry, I won't even hint where. Though believing they might have harmed Gerard's as foolish as thinking I'd want to harm Sophie,' she added, her glance at Luke inimical.

Sophie packed before she went to bed, and dithered about whether to take some of her new clothes. In the end she packed them. They wouldn't be hermits, surely they would be safe going out for the occasional meal, and if not, well, she could dress up occasionally in the evenings.

She packed mostly leisure wear, shorts and jeans, tee shirts and some heavier sweaters in case they were forced to stay until the colder weather came. At the last minute she threw in a swimsuit. Luke had said Cornwall, there might be a chance of swimming in the sea. With a guilty feeling that she ought not to be regarding this as a holiday, she added a camera and a couple of books she'd as yet had no chance to read, made sure she had her new cheque book and passport, all her credit cards, and her more valuable jewellery in her bag. She wondered why she was taking these, but reasoned that she couldn't know what the near future held. She might, for some reason, need to go to Germany, or to see Arlene in Belgium. Or even, she realised, Rod when he'd returned to New York. She hadn't thought about Rod. But there was no way she could get in touch with him now. She'd write to his home address.

She didn't sleep. She was still wide awake, her emotions seesawing between terror at the thought that someone was trying to kill her, and delight at being alone with Luke, when there was a gentle tap at her bedroom door.

'Sophie, are you awake?'

'Come in.'

Luke poked his head round the door. 'I suggest we get straight off and stop for breakfast somewhere on the road. Is your case ready? I've put all my stuff in the car and brought it as close to the kitchen door as possible. You can slip in without being seen, and keep down in the well until we're clear.'

Five hours later Sophie woke to find they were crossing bleak moorland.

'Where are we?'

'Bodmin.'

'I must have slept for ages!'

'You were exhausted, and that big fried breakfast finished you.'

She laughed. 'I meant to share the driving. Are you OK?'

'Not much further to go. Ready for lunch? We can find a pub off the main road, just in case anyone managed to follow us.'

Sophie's eyes clouded over. 'Could they?'

'I don't think so. I didn't use the motorways, it's easier to spot a tail on minor roads. But Pru knows we're in Cornwall. It's possible for someone to trace us.'

'You're not going to start accusing her, are you?' Sophie asked angrily. 'I trust her.'

'All I mean is that she might accidentally give away some clue.'

'Oh. Sorry, I'm paranoid, I can't take all this suspicion of my best friend and my brothers.'

'Forget it. Apart from keeping in touch with Pru once a day you're to forget it. How are your cooking skills?'

'Desperate. I can just about scramble eggs and grill steaks,' Sophie chuckled.

'We'll stop for food in Truro. I'm less likely to see people I know there. Best not to advertise my presence too widely.'

'We'd better get a cook book or two as well if I'm to take over the cooking,' Sophie added cheerfully. 'I always meant to learn, but there was neither time nor the need to, with Mrs Miller around.'

She thought it was as well Luke's car was a large one, when she saw the supplies he considered essential. Trailing him round a supermarket, pushing a second trolley, was a new experience. He went purposefully along every aisle, selecting every possible thing they might need, from washing powder to wine.

'Tins rather than frozen stuff,' he apologised. 'I have a big freezer, but by the time we get there things might have defrosted. We can freeze some vegetables if I buy fresh. What do you like?'

He piled one trolley with tins and household goods, and several boxes of wine and soft drinks, the other with fresh meat and fish, vegetables and fruit. He added biscuits and pasta and rice and bread until Sophie's head was reeling, and she wondered whether he intended to stay until Christmas. They'd never eat all this. Along the way he'd scooped up a dozen of the store's own cook books, and Sophie eyed them with some scepticism. She didn't think she'd have time, even if they stayed there a year, to progress to the sort of luscious gateaux and fancy salads portrayed on the colourful covers.

Luke saw her expression. 'Don't worry,' he said, grinning. 'I'll take my turn too.'

'Where do you get fresh cream and eggs and milk?'

'Local shops or farms. We won't need to go far, or do without.'

'Where is the cottage? South or north coast?' Sophie asked when they were once more in the car.

'It's just to the north of Land's End, overlooking Whitesand Bay. There are some glorious sunsets as it's facing due west.'

'Right by the sea? Wonderful! I've always wanted to live right on the shore.'

'You'll have quite a climb down for that,' he warned.

'Are there many other houses?' she asked.

'Just half a dozen close by, mainly holiday homes, and mostly empty unless someone has rented them out for the whole summer. They are not let on a weekly basis. That will help with keeping our presence reasonably unnoticed, though I very much doubt anyone could find us.'

'I don't think I could find us,' Sophie remarked some time later when Luke turned off the main road onto an unmade track. All she could see was heather stretching to the horizon, and in the distance the sea, glistening in the sunlight.

'Where are the houses? There's nothing

188

between us and the sea.'

'I won't drive over the cliff, I promise.'

The track divided several times, and eventually dipped towards a sheltered hollow on the edge of the cliff. The houses were scattered, none too close to its neighbours, and Sophie's mouth formed an 'O' of delight. Luke drove to the furthest cottage, a square-built stone building with a barn attached, and a small garden surrounded by a thick stone wall, waist high.

Luke got out and opened a field gate, saying that they tried to keep straying animals out, then he opened one of the big doors to the barn and drove straight in. 'We needn't make it too obvious there's anyone here,' he said. 'We can get straight into the kitchen from here.'

Sophie looked round the huge farmhouse kitchen, with a table set at one end, in a square bay window giving a panoramic view of the sea beyond the cliff edge a few yards from the cottage. Luke carried in her case and led her up a twisting flight of stairs to a big landing from which four doors opened.

'This is the bathroom, and the biggest room is next to it, but I use one of the smaller rooms at the front, and you'd probably prefer that too, with the view of the bay.'

The room he showed her was square, with a sloping roof and eaves that jutted well beyond the small window. Despite the bright sun outside it was gloomy, and she had to peer hard to make out the details. The only furniture was a double bed, chests either side of it, and a small dressing table. Bright woven rugs covered the well-polished floorboards, and the floor was slightly uneven, sloping towards the window. Luke opened a cupboard door that had been almost invisible against the heavily patterned wallpaper, and showed her shelves and hanging space.

'No lights apart from the bedside lamps,' he said cheerfully. 'I never got round to installing a lighting circuit upstairs, though there's a bright light in the bathroom, channelled through from below. I didn't think visitors would want to shave or make up in semi-darkness.'

'It's wonderfully peaceful.'

'Put away your stuff while I finish unloading the car, then we'll relax. It's almost time for a gin and tonic.'

'I'll help,' Sophie insisted, and joined

him ferrying cartons from the supermarket into the kitchen. 'Where does everything go?' she asked when the worktops and much of the floor between were almost obliterated by the shopping.

Luke laughed. 'Normally I eat out most of the time, and apart from a loaf, and tea and coffee, I've never had to decide.'

Sophie had been opening cupboards. 'They're mostly empty, so shall I stash everything? Where's the freezer? The meat can go in right away, and I'll do the vegetables tomorrow.'

An hour later, having decided that an omelette was all they intended to cook that evening, they were relaxing with drinks in deep low chairs in front of the sitting room window, staring out at the sky as it slowly turned pink and yellow and pale green on the horizon.

'This is a wonderful place. Why don't you live here all the time instead of London?' Sophie asked lazily.

'Too far away. I need a base in London when I'm doing interviews, or seeing publishers, or promoting my travel books. It takes too long to go by train from Penzance or to drive up, but I try to come as often as possible when I have a long spell of writing to get on with.'

'And when rescued damsels in distress don't take up all your time.'

'I'll have as much time as I want for the next few weeks. Look, I'll cook the supper tonight, do you want to telephone Pru and let her know we've arrived?'

Sophie sighed. 'I suppose I must. I've managed to forget most of the horrors today. I wonder if they've discovered any more?'

They hadn't, yet, she told him when they were sitting in the kitchen, replete with mushroom omelette, cheese and fruit, and having drunk a bottle of wine between them. 'Pru is still fussing, she was cross I hadn't rung the moment we got here, and wanted to know all about this place, whether there were neighbours and so on. She never used to be like this. When we were children it was always Pru who wanted to do mad things, and never mind I was younger, I had to climb the same trees or jump across the same streams or I'd be abandoned. It was determination to keep up with Pru when we were riding that made me jump hedges when I was no more than six and on my first pony. I don't think I'd have attempted it for years longer if it hadn't been for her.'

By ten o'clock Sophie couldn't stop yawning.

'Go to bed,' Luke said, laughing at her. 'We'll go for a walk in the morning, you can explore the beach.' He rose and held out his hand to help her scramble out of the chair. For a moment he held both her shoulders, then he bent and dropped a swift kiss on the end of her nose.

Sleep tight.'

Her eyes filled with sudden tears. 'Dad used to say that,' she explained. 'It's one of the few memories I have of him. No one else has ever said that to me. Good night, Luke, and thank you.'

* * * *

The cry of seabirds woke Sophie just after dawn and she stretched luxuriously. The bed was deliciously soft and she'd slept deeply and dreamlessly. Then the events of the past few weeks swept back into her mind and she sat up, frowning. Someone was trying to kill her, and had succeeded in killing Gerard. For a long time she'd refused to accept this, but could no longer dismiss the odd happenings as accidents.

Gerard's death was murder. She wondered if it was possible that a drip had been contaminated, at fault, or one of the staff had been careless, but taken with all the attacks on her, and the mysterious parcel and poison-pen letter, she knew it was a million to one chance against these all being coincidences. Restless, she went to the bathroom and showered, then pulled on jeans and a thin cotton sweater. She'd leave a note for Luke and go out exploring on her own.

Outside a chill breeze from the sea lifted her hair away from her face. She wandered along the top of the cliff until she came to a well-worn path which snaked down the side of it. It wasn't as steep as she'd expected, there were plenty of slopes where the path vanished and there were clumps of bushes and the occasional patch of turf amongst the shingly surface and the outcrops of rock. At a few steeper parts steps had been hewn to help climbers. There were even, at the steepest or slipperiest sections, a few loops of rope attached to hooks hammered deep in the rocks. Just before the beach proper began there was a jumble of rocks, and Sophie chose a flattish one to sit on. America's out there, she told herself.

There's nothing but sea between me and America. The thought of such vastness made her relax. The gentle rumble of the waves, and the screeches of the gulls, were the only sounds she could hear. She'd always loved seaside holidays as a child, the sharp tang of the salt blown on the wind, the fishy smell of seaweed, and the heat of the sun-warmed rocks. She had a sudden urge to feel the sand between her toes, paddle in the frothy edges of the waves, and recapture those times when death hadn't stalked and terrified her.

Dragging off her sandals she ran, whooping, across the sand and into the shallows. A wave coming in faster than she'd anticipated soaked the legs of her jeans up to the knees, and she gasped at the iciness of it, then laughed aloud, and began to play her childhood game of leaping over the incoming waves. Then unexpectedly her foot slipped on a pebble and she fell headlong into the water, coming up shaking her head, blinking and laughing as she struggled to her feet.

'You can't be left alone for a minute without getting into mischief,' Luke called, and Sophie looked up to see him standing at the edge of the water, aiming a camera at her. 'Come on out, I'm not planning on diving in to rescue you.'

Laughing, she splashed her way towards him, and then bent down and scooped up a handful of water to throw at him. He backed away and she followed, keeping just in the water, until suddenly Luke turned and lunged for her, catching her round the waist before she could evade him. As he swung her up onto his shoulder she collapsed against him, tears of laughter streaming down her cheeks. He carried her a few yards up the sand, then lowered her to the ground, keeping his arms round her.

'I shall exact dire punishment for making me almost as wet as you are,' he said, and before Sophie could move his lips came down on hers, and she was pulled into a strong embrace. His lips tasted of salt. Or perhaps it was her own. Then as suddenly as he had embraced her Luke let her go. 'Come on, breakfast and dry clothes,' he said briskly. 'I'll race you back to the house.'

He was there minutes in front of her, and was sitting on the wall surrounding the garden when she panted up the last stretch of path.

'Unfair,' she declared, collapsing beside him, leaning against the wall. 'I have all these wet clothes to carry, and I had to stop and find my shoes.'

'All's fair in love and war,' he said lightly. 'Coffee and those croissants do you? I'll warm them up while you change. Thank heaven for microwaves.'

'To put me in?' she asked, grinning. She felt so at home with him, she thought. They might have been embarrassed after that sudden embrace, but it had seemed so natural, and he was smiling at her in the same friendly way as ever. She didn't want to begin analysing what it meant, whether it meant anything, or whether they had a relationship which might develop. It was enough to feel happy, free of the grinding worry and pressure that had been with her for weeks, and even the thought of Gerard's death couldn't dim the pleasure of being here in this wonderful place. She would make the most of it, not thinking of either past or future, forgetting everything apart from the present moment.

★ ★ ★ ★

For three days the idyll lasted. Luke

worked for several hours each morning on his book, while Sophie read her novels or searched the cookbooks for recipes she thought she could master for the evening's meal. They usually ate a snack lunch in the garden or down on the beach, and then relaxed in the sun if it was warm enough, or tramped over the clifftops if there was a wind. Luke took hundreds of photographs of her, teasing her that she was becoming vain when she protested at his preference for posing her in unglamorous situations, stuck halfway up a rock she'd tried to climb, or hot and flustered from her attempts at cooking. In the evenings they talked, Sophie eager to find out all she could about Luke.

'With my father being French Canadian I'm bilingual, which helps me to cover interviews with far more people than many journalists can. You'll like my parents. I'll take you to meet them soon.'

He made no further reference to the future, and Sophie thrust all thought of it to the back of her mind. Reality intruded only in the nightly telephone calls to Pru. Karen and Franz, Pru told her, had returned home and would be coming back when Gerard's body was released, to take him back to

Germany for burial. Rod seemed to have disappeared, although there had been a postcard from him, posted in Oxford, showing one of the colleges, but making no mention of Gerard.

'She read it out to me. It was weird. Surely he must know about Gerard! He must have visited the hospital or at least phoned them!'

'Perhaps it's a very intensive course and he has a lot to catch up. He may have sent the postcard before he knew about Gerard. I expect he's been trying to get in touch,' Luke said soothingly.

Then on the third evening Pru telephoned early.

'It's bad, I'm afraid,' she said without preamble. 'I can't spend too long on the phone, I'm expecting the police to come.'

'Police? Why?'

'Oh, come on, Sophie, you must have expected this. The results of the further tests, from the post-mortem, which took longer to do, have come back.'

'And?'

'They've shown it was what Mr Williamson expected, air injected directly into Gerard.'

'Can they be sure?'

'Oh yes, they're sure. I can't remember all the medical terms, but it proves someone murdered him. It wasn't an accident. So of course they want to interview everyone who visited him. Anyone could have had the opportunity if they'd been alone with him. I'm afraid that means you as well, Sophie.'

'We'll come straight back,' Sophie began, but Pru cut in.

'No! That's just what you mustn't do! Can't you see the murderer, whoever it is, will be waiting for that?'

'But the police!'

'I've told the police you've gone away for a short holiday and I don't know where you are, but you'll be back soon. That gives you a few more days, and meanwhile they might discover who it was. If it wasn't Luke Despard!'

'Pru! You know it wasn't!'

'Of course I don't know that, but you wanted to take the risk of being alone with him. At least he hasn't tried to murder you yet. But I didn't want to quarrel. When the police have found the murderer you can come back safely enough.'

Sophie told Luke what Pru had said,

and he suggested they went to the police in Cornwall.

'If we stay in hiding it will look suspicious,' he pointed out. 'We can explain how we feared that you were also a target, and I'm sure they'll understand. One of the police from Wycombe can come here and interview us without our being forced to go back.'

Sophie nodded. 'I suppose so,' she agreed listlessly, but the news had brought back all her problems.

Luke went to her and held her hand. 'Let's go out for a meal, see some normal people for a change.'

She agreed, because she couldn't think of a reason not to. They drove to the south coast, to the Lobster Pot at Mousehole, and it was dark by the time they reached it. Luke held Sophie's hand tucked under his arm as they went into the restaurant. One or two of the local fishermen nodded at Luke, looked curiously at Sophie, and then passed on to join their friends. The holiday season was almost over, and there were only two or three other people who didn't seem to be locals. Despite his best efforts at trying to distract her attention Sophie knew that her period of relaxation had ended. She could not forget her brother's death, and had to face whatever the future held, but she found it difficult to appreciate the food and wine Luke ordered for her.

As they were leaving a man spoke to Luke, asking when he wanted the chimneys of his house pointed.

'I won't be a minute,' Luke apologised, and Sophie nodded and went out in front of him. She strolled across to the edge of the harbour steps and stood peering out to sea, thinking that even when there was no moon it was never completely dark, there were always flashes of light breaking up the surface of the water.

Then she heard footsteps behind her, ringing on the cobbles, and as she turned, thinking it was Luke, was seized by both arms. She saw two men, their faces hidden by masks, and began to struggle wildly, screaming to Luke at the top of her voice. Somehow she broke free and went staggering backwards. She clutched at the air, and screamed again as she felt emptiness all round her, and then her scream was cut off short as she hit the cold water and went under.

Chapter Nine

'Luke, get me away!' Sophie begged. 'I'm afraid they'll try again.'

Dripping wet, cold and shivering, she sat on a wall and tried to avoid looking at the small crowd which had collected when she had, spluttering and coughing, been hauled ignominiously from the water by a couple of brawny fisherman. Why were one's disasters so dreadfully public, she wondered.

'You must be more careful in the dark,' one man was chiding her. 'Losing your step like that was careless, it was.'

'Come into the house and take off those wet clothes,' a woman urged, but Sophie shook her head vehemently.

'I want to go home, and have a hot bath,' she insisted. There were enemies close to her, she didn't dare trust any stranger.

Luke nodded, borrowed a tarpaulin redolent with a fishy aroma, spread it over the back seat of his car, wrapped

Sophie in a rug, and drove swiftly home. She told him, teeth chattering, what had happened.

'Are they following us?' she asked fearfully, craning to see out of the rear window.

'Not another car in sight,' he reassured her. 'They can't approach my cottage without being seen, and in the dark they'd have a devil of a job to find it.'

The journey to the cottage took just a short time, and Luke hurried her inside. 'I'll run a bath, and then make you a hot drink,' Luke said. 'Get those clothes off.'

Shivering, Sophie stripped off her skirt and sweater in her bedroom, and then her bra and briefs. The clinging dampness had gone, but she shivered even more violently, and could scarcely walk to the bathroom, clutching a large bath towel which Luke had slung into her bedroom for her. Luke was bending over the bath, and had poured in so much bath foam the bubbles were in danger of overflowing. He tested the water and nodded.

'Get in, while I make a hot drink. It's not too hot, and there's room to add more hot water as soon as you can stand it. I'll bring the drink up, so don't be modest and lock the door.'

Sophie was past caring about modesty. While she'd resisted being dragged off to a strange house this was different. She dropped the towel and Luke held her arm to steady her as she stepped into the bath. She breathed in sharply.

'Not too hot?' he asked anxiously.

'No, it's wonderful. If this doesn't warm me up nothing will.'

She leant back, and let the warmth steal over her. When Luke came back with the hot chocolate, laced with whisky, she was almost asleep.

'Drink this,' he ordered, sitting down on the side of the bath.

Sophie stretched out her arm. The rest of her was covered with bubbles, and she thought she must look like some TV ad. She sipped the drink, grimacing at the whisky taste, but it did make her feel better, warmer inside.

'Do you feel like talking about what happened?' Luke asked. 'That chap I spoke to does odd building jobs for me, and the first I heard was a commotion and shouts. When we came out to see what was going on you were being plucked from the sea by a couple of stout lads.'

'They tried to grab me. They must have had a car nearby, but I didn't see much,' Sophie said flatly. 'I'd gone over to the harbour, just to look at the sea, and when I began to scream and struggle they let go of me and I stepped back and fell in. They've found me, Luke. They might have been trying to kidnap me, but they could have been trying to kill me instead. I'll never get away.'

'Pru's the only one who has even my telephone number and might know where we are.'

'I don't know what to believe now.'

'I'm in the phone book. She could have looked up the local directory and found the address.'

'Or someone else discovered the number, or even knew you had a cottage here and guessed that's where we'd gone. It's impossible to hide, Luke.'

'No, it isn't. We'll go somewhere else, and this time no one, not even Pru, will know where. Now, are you ready to get out? I've filled a couple of hot water bottles too, and the bed will be warm.'

'I can dry myself, thanks,' she said, making an effort to sound light-hearted as she grinned at him. Luke nodded and left the bathroom. Sophie clambered out of the bath, and within minutes was huddled under the duvet. She heard Luke in the bathroom, and thought guiltily that he'd got wet too from contact with her. But she was sleepy, and her eyes closed, and soon she was fast asleep.

It was the middle of the night when she woke, screaming, a great weight pressing down on her, and the smell of salt water in her nostrils. She struggled, and dimly heard her name being called.

'Sophie, wake up, darling, it's just a dream!'

'What? Oh, Luke, I thought I was drowning!'

'Just a dream,' he soothed, rocking her back and forth. 'Would you like another drink?'

'No. No thanks.' She clutched at him. His arms were bare, and she saw the blond hair on his chest, and the rippling muscles. 'Luke, don't leave me. Please stay with me. I don't want to be on my own.'

'I'll stay till you're asleep again,' he said, reassuringly.

'Hold me. Please.'

The duvet was bulky, and his struggles

to get his arms round her and not uncover her had them both laughing. Sophie tried to sit up.

'I'm sorry. But this is stupid. You'll be so uncomfortable. Get under it with me. Luke,' she added when he hesitated. 'I need you.'

He smiled ruefully and slid under the duvet, and then cradled her in his arms. 'Do you have the slightest idea of the temptation you are?' he asked. 'Go back to sleep, sweetheart, before I forget all my gentlemanly resolutions.'

When she woke again, to full sunlight, he had gone, but the sheet where he'd lain was still warm. Recalling how shamelessly she had made him stay Sophie blushed furiously. What would he think of her? Many of her schoolfriends had live-in boyfriends and she was sure they thought her backward and juvenile because she had never yet made love. Most of the men she'd dated had tried, but she'd been so terrified that it was her money they wanted, and that if she gave way to their persuasions she would somehow be in their power, that she had repulsed their efforts. One part of her, she was sure, had hoped Luke would take advantage of the situation last night. Then she blushed again. Had he imagined she'd planned it all?

She looked at her watch. It was after nine o'clock. She'd better get up and go and look for breakfast. She was trying to decide what to wear when there was a knock on the door.

'Coffee and toast, ma'am,' Luke called, and Sophie sank back into the pillows.

'Come in,' she said, but it was unnecessary. Luke was already in the room, bearing a loaded tray.

'How do you feel?' he asked as he unloaded the contents onto the chest beside the bed.

'Better, thanks, and I'm sorry if I disturbed you last night, with my silly nightmare.'

'It wasn't that which disturbed me,' Luke said, smiling. 'Do you think you'll be fit enough to move today?'

'Move? What—oh. You mean leave here?'

'Yes, for somewhere no one can find us.'

'I'm fine. Yes, I suppose we'll have to go now,' she said regretfully. 'I've loved it here, Luke.'

'Will you be OK for an hour? I need to

go and see the builder, make arrangements for him to keep an eye on the property. And pay him. As soon as I'm back we'll pack up and go. An hotel, this time, I think. Maybe in Wales or as far as Herefordshire.'

Sophie said she'd be fine, and Luke promised to lock all the doors. 'Keep away from the windows. I'll be as quick as I can.'

As soon as he'd gone Sophie scrambled into some clothes and ran downstairs. She might catch Pru at home. She was lucky. Mrs Miller answered at the second ring, and Sophie cut into her exclamations by demanding to speak to Pru at once if she was anywhere near.

'In the stables, love. I'll go and give her a shout.'

Sophie hopped from one foot to the other as she waited, and breathed a sigh of relief when she heard the phone being picked up.

'Sophie? It's Pru. How are you?'

'Pru, I haven't got long. Have you told anyone where we are?'

Pru laughed, and Sophie could detect the bitterness in her voice. 'Fat chance when I don't know myself! Why? Has anything happened?'

'Have you given anyone else the phone number? Or left it on the pad by the phone, perhaps?'

'Of course not. Sophie, what's the matter?'

Sophie Was suddenly reluctant to tell her. 'Nothing,' she muttered. 'It's just—I thought I saw someone yesterday, looking at the house oddly, suspiciously,' she invented. 'I must have been imagining things. How are things at home?'

'Not so good,' Pru admitted. 'The police have been very persistent, want to find you. I really do think they suspect Luke. When they discovered about your father's money, how it was left, they even began to suspect you.'

'Me? They think I could kill my own brother?' Sophie demanded, shocked.

'They suspect everybody. And you must confess you've got a motive, in their eyes. You'll have a lot of explaining to do when you come back, unless they've found someone else to pin it on instead of Luke. And that doesn't look likely, they've eliminated everyone else who saw Gerard that last day. Are you absolutely sure he wasn't alone with Gerard? A few seconds would have been enough. Even if you had your back to him for a while he could have done it. Sophie, I don't like to think of you alone with him. Anything could happen.'

'I must go,' Sophie said. She didn't want to have the same arguments all over again. Yet after she put the phone down Pru's words remained with her. Luke had, in theory, had the opportunity for carrying out all the attacks. He could even have pushed her in last night, it might not have been an attempted kidnap. They could have hoped she'd hit her head on a boat or a rock and it would appear an accident. It was her good fortune she hadn't and someone had rescued her. She went upstairs to pack her case. She ought to go down to Mousehole and try to discover whether Luke had been talking to the builder all the time, until after she'd fallen in. But she wouldn't know if they were telling her the truth. If it were Luke he'd had an accomplice. There might have been two others. He had to have at least one to drive the Volvo which had started off the whole ghastly business. How could she trust anyone? And on top of it all the police were suspicious of her, searching for her, ready, apparently, to charge her with murdering her own brother.

Suddenly she made up her mind. She was surrounded by people she couldn't trust. Rod had vanished, and he was the only one who would benefit from her death now that Gerard was dead. Pru would get the rest of the business, but that hardly seemed worth killing for, and she could not have carried out most of the attacks. She'd need to be working with others too. But what was Luke's motive? Could he possibly be working with Rod? It wasn't possible. Or with Pru? That was even more unlikely. They'd made it clear they didn't like one another. Or they'd pretended not to.

She was on her own. She was the only person she could trust, and somehow she had to find her own way out of this mess.

★ ★ ★ ★

'We'll stop for lunch somewhere near Bristol,' Luke said as they drove over the Tamar bridge.

Sophie nodded. That would suit her very well. She could get a train, and would soon be in Oxford. 'Where are you going?' she asked.

'Where would you prefer? If we keep moving every day or so, as if we're touring, we'll be less noticeable, and so long as we keep away from the Thames Valley area we should be safe enough.'

She lay back and closed her eyes, pretending to be asleep. It hurt too much to talk to Luke, to know that she would soon be leaving him. These last few days had been so perfect, despite the threat that hung over them. She'd begun to wonder whether she was in love with him, and had relished every slight contact, when his arm touched hers or his hand brushed against her face in that tender, caressing way he had. She tried to recall the sensation of their closer moments, when he'd kissed her on the beach that day she'd been fooling about and fell into the sea, and especially lying in his arms last night. At that time she'd have welcomed him eagerly if he'd made love to her. She'd been hoping for it, she admitted, and stole a glance at his profile through her lashes.

He couldn't possibly want to harm her! It was ridiculous to imagine for a moment that he'd attacked her last night. What possible motive could he have? When she came to think about it rationally, the only possible motive could be that he was working for Rod, yet she found that difficult to believe too. Rod didn't want her inheritance. And just supposing Luke was in league with him, they'd have to share the money whereas—and her heart gave a leap at the very idea—if Luke married her he'd have it all, her share of the stables too. And after a suitable interval he could kill her, another accident, and inherit it all.

Perhaps he was already married. It was strange that so attractive a man, in his late twenties, should still be single, after all. Even if he was, divorce was easy these days, she argued with herself He'd only have to wait. And yet these past few days, despite their surface happiness, he'd withdrawn. He'd rarely touched her deliberately, and there had been hundreds of opportunities for him to make love to her. When she'd touched him, taking his arm or catching his hand in hers, he'd removed himself out of reach as soon as he could. Didn't he want her?

The thoughts churned round in her mind, and she became even more confused. By the time Luke pulled into the car park of a large pub a few miles short of Bristol she had a raging headache. She'd eat first, she decided, before making her escape. It would help her headache. It would also, though she hastily thrust aside this thought, allow her to spend another hour with Luke.

In the end she wondered if she'd been wise. The extra hour was a peculiar form of torture. Luke had done various stories in different parts of Wales, and he told her of the places they could visit. Sophie tried to pretend an interest, but was beyond feigning decisions as to their movements.

'I've never been to Wales, it will all be new to me,' she said at last when he was pressing her for an opinion.

'Then let's go.' He signalled for the bill, and Sophie took a deep breath and stood up.

'I'll just go to the loo,' she said, 'see you out by the car.'

Luckily he couldn't see the corridor to the cloakrooms from the dining room, so Sophie could turn the other way and head for the front door. Behind the pub was a rambling housing estate built in the fifties, and with mature hedges and trees in the gardens. Once outside the

216

pub she clutched her handbag, into which she'd packed bare essentials, and ran. Five minutes, she reckoned, before he'd start searching for her, and she needed to get as far away as she could before hiding.

Soon she was forced to drop into a walk, despite the slope of the road. In the distance she could see a gleam of water, the Bristol Channel. She walked as fast as she could, with short bursts of running, as she wove her way through the virtually empty streets. After three slow minutes she could bear the tension no longer, wanting to look behind her at every step to see whether Luke's car was visible, and began to search for a suitable garden in which to hide. She spotted one almost at once, a wide plot with a small detached house, and lots of overgrown evergreen shrubs. A couple of pints of milk were still on the doorstep. With luck the owners would be at work, and people in the neighbouring houses could see little in the garden.

She looked all round, but there was no one in sight apart from an old man with a dog a long way back, facing the other way, so she slipped through the open gates and plunged into the bushes which formed a thick, ragged and straggly hedge.

Sophie slowly pushed her way along, always moving towards the back of the house, until she came to a clump of rhododendron and crept beneath the all-concealing foliage. He would never find her here.

How long would he search for her? He might wait all day, cruising round in his car. After all, he hadn't an urgent appointment to get to. Her plan, born of desperation, seemed totally impracticable now. She waited for an hour, getting more and more nervous, and then heard a new sound from the road beyond the garden which backed on to this one. It was a large vehicle, a diesel engine and it sounded like a bus toiling up the slope on which the estate was built.

Abandoning caution, Sophie fought her way out of the bushes and ran for the fence at the end of the garden. Luckily it was no more than waist high, and she threw herself over, landing on a smoothly mown lawn in a garden full of raised flower beds newly planted with pansies. As she picked herself up and raced for the pathway at the side of the house a woman appeared at the kitchen door.

'Hey, what's going on? How dare you trespass in my garden!'

Sophie hesitated. If she didn't give the woman some explanation she might cause trouble, phone the police, even chase her. 'I—I'm running away from my boyfriend,' she gasped. 'I'm sorry I came through your garden, but I'm so scared he'll hit me again. I need to get the Bristol bus. Isn't that it, just coming?'

The woman nodded. 'There's a stop just outside,' she said, 'but I don't understand—'

Sophie smiled. 'Thanks. You've saved my life!' She ran.

The bus ground to a halt as she puffed towards the stop. Sophie waited impatiently while two women with baby buggies and, it seemed, half a dozen children apiece, clambered aboard. Every second she expected to see Luke's car draw up behind her, but eventually she was able to get on herself. For the first time that day she felt able to relax. By great good fortune the bus was going to Bristol, but it meandered through country lanes, stopping at what seemed like endless villages, before Sophie was able to alight at the station. She hurried through, and had only a quarter of an hour to wait for a train. She'd half expected to find Luke waiting for her, but though she peered round anxiously saw no one even slightly resembling him. By the time she was on the train she could think about her next moves.

Sophie had to change trains at Didcot, but she reached Oxford before the shops closed. Providing herself with luggage and clothes was the first priority. She made for the Westgate shopping centre, bought herself a small rucksack, and then equipped herself with underclothes, a track suit, trainers, a pair of jeans and a couple of sweaters. She added a good skirt and blouse, and on reflection a smart pair of shoes and tights. She had no idea where she might have to go in the next few days, and needed to be prepared for everything. Belatedly she recalled that she didn't even have her anorak with her, she'd had to abandon that in the car, so she went looking for another, and at the last moment, when the store's staff were beginning to look impatient, added a jacket to wear with the skirt.

Even wearing one of the sweaters and the anorak, it was difficult to crush everything into the rucksack, but eventually she managed it, and set off to find somewhere to stay. Any large hotel was out. She looked like a student, so for the time being a small hotel would serve her purpose. Bed and breakfast places, she decided, would have curious proprietors. And she wanted to be as close to the city centre as possible. Then she remembered the motel out on the bypass. It wasn't in the city, but it would take ages to find a suitable place to stay and it would soon be getting dark. The motel would be ideal, anonymous, with cafes in the nearby service station, and the Park and Ride bus virtually next door. Sophie debated how to get there and plumped for a taxi. She'd had enough of buses and might have to wait for ages. And if the motel should have no spare rooms she'd have to start all over again. A taxi driver would have some suggestions.

She was lucky. At the Welcome Lodge a room had just been cancelled, so she booked in for a week, deposited her rucksack, decided to avoid the restaurant, and then went to the nearby shop to buy sandwiches, biscuits, a bottle of mineral water and a paperback novel to read. She added a guide book to Oxford and a newspaper. In Cornwall they hadn't even listened to the radio, and she wanted to know if there was a big search for her and Luke, whether Gerard's death was a big story.

There was a brief report on an inside page, which she found on her second, more careful search. No one had yet been charged with the murder, but the police were concerned about the disappearance of the victim's cousin, who had left her home some days ago with a family friend, on a visit from France, who was also wanted by the police for questioning. Sophie stared at the report. She'd never before had experience of press inaccuracy, and for a moment felt aggrieved. Then she grinned. It might be as well they'd got it wrong, might help her in her plans.

She ate the sandwiches, made some coffee, and tried to read, but after two pages during which she took in not a single word, gave up and let her mind wander over the events of the past few weeks. She needed to try and sort out her ideas, and she needed to write things down. She sat down once more to make a list on the blank pages at the back of her paperback of what had happened, and when, and then another list of Oxford colleges.

That made her pause. She intended

approaching them all, asking if Rod had been on any course, and if possible trying to trace him that way. But the police could have been there before her. They might be waiting for her. She needed to disguise herself. Hair, she thought. First thing in the morning I'll have to do something to my hair.

It was long after midnight before Sophie slept. She kept imagining Luke was beside her, his arms round her in a comforting embrace. And she wanted to feel his hard muscles against her body, she wanted him to kiss her, to caress her in ways he'd never begun to do, despite the opportunities he'd had. He'd called her darling, and sweetheart, but they were words one might use to a child, encouraging them not to be afraid. He'd kissed her, a couple of times, but he'd made no attempt to follow up these advances, even though she must have made it obvious to him that she'd have welcomed more. Hadn't he wanted to? If he was working for someone, aiming to kill her, his restraint was explained. Yet most men, having her in their power as Luke had done, would have tried to take advantage of the situation. Wouldn't they?

She sighed and turned over. She didn't know much about men. She'd been wary of them for so long, had never trusted anyone so much as she had Luke, and now she was highly suspicious about him. She wondered what he was doing now. Had he searched for her for long? Had he gone to the police? Would the police in Bristol as well as the ones at home be looking for her? With a jolt she realised that the Thames Valley Police Headquarters was no more than a few miles away, at Kidlington. Had the police arrested Luke? Had he gone back to Crispins, assuming she might be heading there? Or was he, guilty of what she suspected, in hiding somewhere? Had he got rid of her luggage, of all trace of her, and headed for Wales as they'd planned to do together? Or was he with whoever it was he was working for, making further plans to find and kill her?

She slept at last, dreaming she was falling again into the dark water of the harbour, coming up close to a boat and clutching at the side of it, then fighting as she found someone in the water alongside her, only to be clasped in iron-hard arms and hauled out onto the quay. In the morning, weary, she forced herself out of bed and under the shower, dressed in her jeans and one of the new sweaters, gulped a cup of black powdered coffee, and slung her anorak over her shoulder. It looked as though it was going to rain soon. She stuffed the sheet she'd torn from the paperback with her list of colleges into her bag and went out to catch the Park and Ride bus into the city centre.

She got off by the Martyrs' Memorial and went in search of a hairdresser. Three hours later she emerged, her already short hair cut even shorter, this time in a spiky effect instead of the smooth cap it had been, and an indistinctive shade of mouse. She found some cheap reading glasses that didn't distort her vision too much, but changed her appearance even more, and decided to add dangly earrings. In the cloakroom of Debenham's she put on the bright scarlet lipstick she'd purchased, and grimaced at her reflection. She doubted if even Pru would recognise her. Suddenly she felt ravenously hungry, and decided that a good lunch now would mean she could make do again this evening with sandwiches in her room, so she went to the store restaurant and chose her food. She sat at a table overlooking the street, and let her mind drift onto her plans. She was tired of running away. Rod was the only person who would benefit from Gerard's death and hers, so she would find him and confront him. He'd been behaving oddly, he needed to explain that. And if he could prove his innocence, as she hoped, they would be together to search for the real villain who had been terrorising her and had killed their brother.

Chapter Ten

Broad Street was right opposite, beyond the St Mary Magdalen Church, and Sophie decided to start there. She'd tackle the colleges in the centre first, then try the more outlying ones. It took considerable persistence to penetrate beyond the gates, and find someone who both could and would look up lists of attendees at summer courses. By the end of the afternoon Sophie had covered only four colleges and was feeling depressed. It was a hopeless task. There were over thirty to do, and various specialist institutes. When she realised that she'd have the morning too the following day, Sophie cheered up. If she could do eight in a day, she might cover them all in a week, and anyway she might soon be lucky and trace the one Rod had been to.

She was exhausted from tramping about, and seemed to be developing a cold. Her throat had an ominous tickle. This time her shopping, as well as food for the evening, included throat lozenges and aspirin and more tissues. She couldn't afford to be ill.

There was no mention of her or Gerard in today's paper, so perhaps the police were not looking for her. They could only know she was missing if Luke had reported it. Correction, she thought, they'd already been looking for her. She was feeling muzzier by the minute, so she undressed, put on her new tracksuit over her new pyjamas, and took herself to bed where she nibbled cheese sandwiches and tried to work out a logical route to follow the next day.

She slept heavily, and in the morning had so severe a headache she couldn't even face coffee. A couple of aspirins helped slightly, but it was after ten before she was feeling fit enough to dress and go once more into Oxford. Once more she trailed round the colleges, and by four wondered whether she was being totally stupid, whether she should give in and call Pru to come and fetch her. At home she'd be able to rest, and she almost didn't care if the police threw her into prison.

She'd worked her way into the High Street, and just emerged from Queen's when a wave of dizziness swept over her. She staggered towards the wall and sat on a ledge, leaning forward with her head between her knees.

'Are you OK?'

It was a thin man about thirty, with a beard and heavy spectacles, who was eyeing her apprehensively.

'Just faint,' Sophie replied. 'I'll be OK in a minute.'

He sat beside her, putting an old canvas bag bulging with books and papers on the ground between them. 'I'm afraid I overheard what you were asking the porter,' he said hesitantly. 'I think I may have been on the same course, tutoring it, that is.'

Sophie's head came up sharply, and she swayed against him. 'Oh, I'm sorry. You were? I'm trying to find my brother, Rod

228

Stein, but I don't know which college the course was at. They said it wasn't here.'

'No. Actually it was at Brookes, the new University, you know, which used to be the Polytechnic. Out at Headington.'

Sophie stood up and swayed again. 'I must go there straight away! Is there a bus?'

'You're not fit to go anywhere,' the young man said with sudden resolution. 'Why not have a cup of tea with me, and tell me what it's about. My name's Alan Davis. I'm a tutor at Queen's. There's a cafe just along here.'

He took her arm and steered her further along the street, then turned into a small cafe and made her sit down at a table near the window. Without consulting her he ordered tea and sandwiches and cakes, and Sophie realised she had eaten nothing all day. Gratefully she took a sandwich. She was getting tired of sandwiches, but they were easy and fast and she promised herself she'd have a proper meal later that night. She fished out the aspirins from her bag and swallowed two. She'd forgotten to take those too.

'Better?' Alan asked.

'Thanks. Yes. The course, what was it?

Rod works in a bank in New York.'

'International trade, payments and bills and futures and such stuff,' he said briskly. 'Rod told me he wanted to specialise in that area.'

'You knew him? Do you have any idea where he is now?'

'He was going straight back to New York. He'd been off sick for some time, he said, and almost didn't make the course. It was quite a strain, I believe, he missed a couple of days, but I gave him a copy of my notes for those lectures and he said he'd be able to get the rest from some of the other people. He said that one of the days he'd been to see his brother.'

'Can you remember which days?' Sophie asked.

Alan pulled out a diary and flipped through it. 'Let me see. Yes, look, he missed my second lecture, on the Wednesday. I'm afraid I don't know the other day, it was just that he said he'd missed some more when I spoke to him at the end of course party.'

Sophie was feeling cold. That Wednesday was the day Gerard had been knocked off his bike. And it sounded possible that Rod could have been at the Oxford

230

hospital on the day Gerard was killed. 'He's back in New York?' she asked.

'Yes, I said so. Forgive me, but you don't sound American.'

'Rod's my half-brother, we have different mothers and I was brought up in this country while he stayed in the States. Thank you for your help. Please will you let me pay for the tea?'

'Of course not. Where are you staying? I don't like the idea of your going on a bus alone.'

Nor did Sophie, her legs were feeling decidedly odd. 'At the Welcome Lodge, by the Peartree roundabout,' she said. 'Do you think I could get a taxi? Would they be able to phone for one from here?'

'I'll do it. And if I may, I'll share it with you. I live near there, just off Five Mile Drive, so it's only a short walk back. I'd feel much happier if I made sure you were safely home.'

Sophie slept for a couple of hours, and though, when she woke, she didn't want a meal, she forced herself to go the few yards to the Little Chef next door, and order hot food. Even chips, she thought, were better than her diet of sandwiches, but she was wary of using the Lodge restaurant where she might be remembered.

The following day she felt too ill to move, and spent most of the day in the room, going out just to buy food and newspapers and lots of soft drinks to soothe her aching throat. She'd meant to telephone Rod, but decided she was too lightheaded to concentrate on what she wanted to say. What could she do next?

The problem was too much, but when she woke early on the next day she felt almost back to normal. She went to the cafe and had a good breakfast, and while she ate decided that the next step was to try and trace Gerard's movements. He'd been in England for some time, Karen had told her, visiting friends while the rest of the family went to Australia. But who were they? And what could they tell her? At least it wasn't too early to telephone Karen. But when she got through a strange voice told her that *'Herr und Frau Hoffmann gehen sie nach England,'* and Sophie could learn no more. She considered ringing Pru, but that might be foolish. Pru must have betrayed their hideaway to someone, if it had not been Luke who attacked her.

It would be some time before she could

ring Rod, so she began to go through all the possibilities once more.

Luke first. She had to eliminate Luke. He could not have been the man in the Volvo. But he had been there, very conveniently, in order to rescue, or appear to rescue her. He could have done all the other things, the attempted kidnap, tried to run her over with the motorbike, and push her from the tube platform. He couldn't have killed Gerard, because he'd never been alone with him, that last day. Then she went cold. She'd just recalled something. As they'd left the ward and she had stopped to speak to the Sister, Luke had excused himself. She'd assumed he wanted to visit the loo. But he could just as easily have slipped back into the ward. And he might have pushed her into the harbour at Mousehole.

Luke was a possibility, though the fact remained that his motive was weak.

Now for Rod. She didn't know where he'd been. He'd told Alan he'd been off work sick for some time. How long? She hastily counted on her fingers. Surely not for almost two months before Gerard died? But the girl at the bank had told Luke he was on vacation for a week, then on the course. She'd said nothing about sick leave. So Luke had said. She hadn't heard that for herself. Then Rod had told her he'd taken a place at the last minute. It didn't add up. He wasn't the man in the Volvo either, for she'd seen his face briefly. But why hadn't he phoned as he'd promised? And how could he have known she was in Cornwall? Had he visited Gerard the last day? She thought the hospital had said so. When did he go back to the States? She needed to ask some questions, but how could she when showing her face might mean she was arrested herself?

No one else had a motive for murdering Gerard, but the way the trust had been set up meant that only the surviving siblings could benefit.

Suddenly she recalled the hospital saying a young couple had visited Gerard. Who were they? She'd assumed it was the friends he'd been staying with, who had somehow heard about his accident. That meant they probably lived near Wycombe and read the local paper. Otherwise, who could have told them? His parents? It wasn't likely, they were too worried to make such phone calls. Rod? That was more likely, though she still didn't understand how Rod himself had been reading the Wycombe paper. Perhaps one of the students, a local person on his course had taken it in, and had noticed that he had the same name.

There were too many questions, but at least Alan Davis might be able to answer some of them. Luckily he had written down his address and his home and college phone numbers. She could ring him. She tried both numbers but neither answered. She looked at her watch, and decided to try Rod. It would be six, or nearly so, in New York. Again no answer.

Back to thinking. She hadn't considered Pru yet. Pru had no possible cause to kill Gerard, though Sophie suddenly recalled that Pru had been away from Crispins that day for a couple of hours. That would have been long enough to visit the hospital. Where had she been? Yes, Aylesbury, in the opposite direction to Oxford. But she hadn't said what she was doing, so there was no way Sophie could check. And back to the old question of motive. Pru knew well enough how Peter Stein's money had been left. Her only motive could be the rest of the business. And without an accomplice to carry out most of the attacks it couldn't be Pru. Who could have been her accomplice? Yet it must have been Pru who'd told someone Sophie was in Cornwall.

Sophie went back to the telephone, but again they were all non-communicative. She'd always been suspicious of the detective books she read where the sleuth was always connected straight away to the people he telephoned. They were never at work, out at lunch, away on holiday, off sick, or just not there. It made real life detection far more difficult.

By twelve she could stand the inactivity no longer. She'd go to Brookes University and try to find someone else who might have been on the course, perhaps some local students, or maybe another tutor like Alan. She'd wear the good skirt and jacket and take a taxi, she was tired of buses, and besides it was out of the centre, too far to walk according to her map, and there were several buildings.

It was a fruitless journey. All the students had been from abroad or London, she was told. They would not release any of the addresses of the London students to her. None of the tutors from the course were around. They were all from different colleges, and term hadn't begun yet for most of them.

She asked the taxi-driver to take her to Alan Davis's house. As they stopped outside she saw his thin figure putting the key in the door. He turned, and Sophie almost fell out of the taxi in her anxiety.

'Alan, wait!' She paid off the taxi, and ran up the short drive.

'Hi, there. Are you better?'

'Much, thanks.'

'I did think about coming to see you, but I had a lot to do yesterday, and I didn't know your room number. Why don't you come in and have a drink?'

'Thanks, I'd like that.'

He led her into a room cluttered with ancient armchairs, and a huge old-fashioned oak dining table on which were a computer and precariously piled heaps of books and folders. In the alcoves on either side of the fireplace bookshelves reached to the ceiling, most of them sagging under the weight of the tomes crammed into them.

'Like some coffee?' he asked, and Sophie saw a filter machine on a side table. She nodded, and Alan reached down a couple of mugs from a Welsh dresser and filled them. 'I keep it on all day,' he explained.

'I depend on caffeine, and it means I don't have to keep going out to the kitchen for more. Is black OK? I do have some milk.'

'Black's fine,' Sophie said, and took a sip. It was incredibly strong, and stewed from sitting on the filter hotplate. She glanced surreptitiously round for a handy pot plant and saw an unidentifiable, wilting specimen on the windowsill. Even this coffee wouldn't harm it too badly, she decided.

'Did you get in touch with Rod?' Alan asked, gulping his coffee with evident enjoyment.

'I felt too ill yesterday to care. I tried to phone before I went out this morning, but there was no one there. And it was too early to try his office. I've been trying to contact some of the other tutors, but there was no luck there either. Do you know who they were, and whether they'd talk to me?'

'I can do better than that. I was working late last night, so I phoned Rod myself after he'd have got home from work.'

'Is he there? When did he go home? What did he say?'

'I didn't speak to him, but there was a girl there.'

'A girl? I didn't know Rod had a live-in girlfriend. What did she say?'

'Just that he'd be back later. So I left a message and asked him to ring back and say when he'd be in for you to contact him. Gave this number, as I didn't know if it would be possible for him to get you at the motel. I knew I could leave a message there for you. And anyway, I've got an answering machine. I haven't listened to it yet.'

'May I?' Sophie asked, looking round for the phone.

Alan grinned at her. 'I keep it in the kitchen, and leave the machine on all the time. I hate being interrupted when I'm trying to work. Come on, let's go and listen.'

He headed for the door. Sophie hastily baptised the plant with her coffee, set down the mug and followed him out. He was looking at the telephone, but no lights blinked at them.

'No messages, I'm afraid,' he said. 'I'll play back the last just to make sure.'

He did so, and it was just an old message.

Sophie's shoulders drooped. 'Thanks, Alan. You've done a lot more than necessary.'

'I wanted to help. Look, why don't I take you to see some of the other tutors, and then we could go out for a meal.'

Sophie didn't feel like being sociable, but he'd helped so much she hadn't the heart to say no to the meal. 'Thanks, I'd like that.'

'Good. Look, I'll just phone those fellows and make sure they'll be in, then we can go.'

They saw two, an elderly, vague man who seemed much more like an Oxford don to Sophie than Alan did, and an incredibly brisk woman in an orange leotard which clashed wildly with her scarlet hair, who talked to them while she did vigorous exercises on an awesome-looking rowing machine. Neither of them knew anything about Rod, they hadn't even been aware of his absences on some days.

'Is there anyone else?' Sophie asked bleakly as they left the woman's flat in a newish block between the Banbury and Woodstock roads. 'Is there any way of tracing some of the students? I was told some of them lived in London, but they wouldn't give me any addresses.'

'They wouldn't, but I might be able to find out for you. Come on, I'll take you to the Crypt, it's an Oxford institution. We can catch a bus along the Woodstock Road.'

'Would you? Find the addresses, I mean?'

'I can try. There's just one thing. You know Rod's at home, it's just a matter of waiting until you can find him in. Why do you need to talk to people on the course?'

Sophie bit her lip. Alan had been so helpful she hadn't expected him to start asking awkward questions. She thought rapidly. 'Our brother—well, half-brother to both of us, by my father's third wife, died while he was over here. I know he went to see Gerard, and I wanted to know how he felt, whether Gerard had regained consciousness, talked to him at all.'

She felt terrible making up these lies for Alan, but he seemed to accept them. They were silent on the short bus journey, and until Alan had steered her along a narrow alley off Cornmarket and down some steep stairs into what had once been the crypt of an old church he didn't speak apart from casual remarks. Over dinner, in the dim, candle-lit rooms which all seemed to lead out of one another into far distant and even dimmer regions, he asked about her life and she told him about the stables, but mentioned nothing of the strange attacks that had been made on her.

Alan insisted on getting a taxi back to the motel, saying that buses were difficult at that time of night, and she shouldn't try to walk too far in the dark, along what was in parts a lonely road. 'I'll just wait and make sure you get inside all right, then the taxi can take me home,' he added.

Sophie was feeling exhausted. She hadn't properly recovered from her cold, and wanted nothing except a hot bath and bed. She could wait until tomorrow to decide on further plans, if she could think of anything constructive to do. On the journey out from Oxford, sleepy from the good food and wine, she almost slept.

Alan spoke as they drew up outside the motel. 'I'll see you in the morning, let you know if Rod phoned. How about us having breakfast together? It's ages since I had a good fry-up, and we could go to the Little Chef or the other cafe. Would nine suit you?'

'Thanks. That would be a good idea. I hope Rod doesn't telephone you in the middle of the night.'

She went towards the block and at the top of the outer stairs turned to wave to Alan. His taxi was already turning round and she watched it leave. He was nice. And he'd been so helpful. He appeared to live alone, and she thought he didn't have many friends. He'd talked about his teaching, but seemed to have no outside interests. When she'd asked him about his own life he'd implied that he spent most of the time working. Pressed, he remembered going to a film or a concert occasionally, but admitted he didn't take much advantage of the many university social activities. He was probably shy and lonely.

She walked along the open passageway to her room and let herself in. The lights were on, the window open judging by the billowing curtains which were drawn over them, and Luke was stretched out on the bed, fast asleep.

Sophie's heart missed a beat. He'd found her. He looked so handsome, and she didn't know whether her emotions were gladness to see him again or fear that he intended her harm. She took a step back towards the door, then sighed deeply. If he could trace her here was there any point in running away from him? She had nowhere to go. She could run to Alan and beg his help, but then she'd have to explain everything to him, and he'd never believe her. She was too tired to make the effort to try and convince him.

She moved further into the room, dropping her jacket and bag on the chair beside the dressing table. Then she stood looking down at Luke. He was pale, and his breathing was heavy. Was he just tired? And how had he managed to get into her room? Had he sweet-talked the receptionist into letting him have a key? If he had she'd make a big fuss, but not now. She hadn't the energy.

Suddenly she wanted desperately to lie down beside him, to go to sleep. This time, though, he wouldn't hold her in his arms. She'd welcomed his warmth and comfort then, but she daren't trust him again until she was sure he was on her side, not working for that unknown enemy. She sat down on the side of the bed. Why didn't he wake up? Then she could find out how he had found her, and insist he slept on the small settee which could be made into a child's bed. He would be uncomfortable, but serve him right. She shook her head. She was being ridiculous. There was probably another room available, and he would have to go there. But if he meant her harm, he wouldn't risk letting her escape. Sophie retrieved her jacket and pulled it on. However tired she was, she had to get away. She couldn't take a chance on Luke's motives. Briefly she wondered whether she might pack her case. He looked deeply asleep, but the wardrobe door made a squeaking noise which would probably wake him. She daren't risk that, and she daren't risk going into the bathroom even for her toothbrush.

Fortunately her important possessions were all in her bag, her money, passport and jewels. She never risked leaving them behind. With a last lingering look at Luke she turned towards the door and gasped. The bathroom door was opening. It had been closed when she came past it. The light from the main room showed her a shadow in the doorway. Then the shadow moved and Sophie moved backwards. She hadn't time to reach the phone. If she screamed, would anyone hear her? Her room looked out over the back, not the car park in front of the motel, and she didn't know what was out there.

It seemed hours before the figure emerged, and Sophie stared, terrified. She had no weapon, nothing to use to defend herself. They'd caught her at last, she thought wildly. The people who'd killed Gerard had caught her now, and they wouldn't let her live.

Then she tripped, moving backwards, and collapsed onto the end of the bed. The figure in the doorway chuckled, and an answering laugh came from behind him. There were two of them. It seemed to make it worse. She might have had some hope with just one of them, and if by some miracle Luke was on her side, and woke up, they might have had a chance.

She watched, helpless, as they emerged fully. They wore black jeans and polo-necked sweaters, but the worst thing was the masks over their faces. She shivered as she recalled the other faceless men who'd terrorised her. They were both short and dark haired, but that was the only thing she could see. She would never be able to identify them even if she came out of this alive. They were broad shouldered and muscular, and moved with the grace of athletes. They came to stand at the foot of the bed, to either side of her as she sat watching, mesmerised.

'Home at last, darling,' the slightly taller one said. 'Have you been painting the town red?'

At last Sophie found her voice. 'Who the devil are you and what are you doing in my room? How did you get in?'

'You don't want to bother your pretty little head about that,' he replied. 'Pack.'

'What?'

'Pack, I said. Unless you want to spend the next I don't know how many days in the same clothes. Even a dainty puss like you can get stinking after a few days. Move!'

Sophie complied. At least they didn't mean to kill her right now, and there might be opportunities to escape. They probably meant to take her where they could stage some sort of show, make her death appear to be an accident. She vowed to herself that she would do all she could to foil them, and she would certainly try to leave traces of a struggle.

She soon had her rucksack packed, and looked to see whether the activity had woken Luke, but he was as deeply asleep as ever, which was odd. The smaller man took her rucksack and went to the door.

'Walk,' the spokesman said. 'Follow him and don't try to make a run for it or scream, or I'll break your arm.'

He took her arm in a vice-like grip and marched her out of the room. They met no one, and immediately outside she was bundled into the back of a large car. Then she felt a prick in her arm, and knew no more.

Chapter Eleven

Sophie was stiff and cold. She wriggled her shoulders and winced. She seemed to be lying on hard boards and her whole body ached intolerably. Her eyelids felt incredibly heavy and it was difficult to open them, but after a few minutes she managed it. There was a faint blob of light to one side, and gradually she decided that it was a window. Her head felt muzzy, but she was by now awake enough to know that she was lying partly on a rough woollen mat with her head and shoulders on bare, polished floorboards. She tried to sit up and found it difficult to move, then it dawned on her that her feet were trussed together at the ankles, and her arms behind her back.

Suddenly she felt furiously angry, and the surge of adrenalin helped her to roll onto her front and struggle onto her knees. It had been getting lighter, and she could distinguish different shapes in the room. There was a chest of drawers underneath the window in front of her, a wardrobe, leaning drunkenly, to her left, and a high, metal-framed bed on her right. She twisted her head round and saw that the door behind her was closed. And Luke, trussed as she was herself, was sprawled across the bed.

'Luke?' she whispered, but he did not respond and she had a moment's panic that he was dead. How could she have doubted him? Whoever was trying to kill her had now got them both. The only surprise was that she was still alive. If they were the same people who had killed Gerard why had they gone to the bother of keeping her a prisoner? Gradually the events of her capture were coming back to her. Luke had been asleep on the bed in her motel room. She'd assumed he had found her, but now it looked as though her captors, whoever they were, had put him there and then, when she was secured, brought them both here. She recalled the prick in her arm which was her last memory. They'd given her something which had knocked her out. They must have done the same to Luke. She struggled against the fog in her brain. Somehow they had found Luke first. If they'd given him some injection too they wouldn't have felt safe leaving him outside the motel while they waited for her. They had a car in which he'd be visible, not a van. And in her room, sedated, he needn't be tied up.

She looked at him again. He was breathing more easily than last night, but he must have been out for longer than she had. 'Luke, wake up!' she said, louder, and leant forward to where she could nudge the bed with her shoulder. His eyelids flickered, and she breathed a sigh of relief.

A sound from below stopped her relief. She'd almost forgotten the men who had captured them. They'd both worn masks, she recalled, until they'd got in the car.

She hadn't caught even a glimpse of their features. It had been risky, they might have met someone, but she supposed that if they had, they'd have been able to whip off the masks. They must have carried Luke, but again they could have pretended he was a friend, dead drunk, and they were taking him home. Who would bother to query that, in an impersonal place like a motel?

Steps sounded outside the room, running up wooden stairs, and the door burst open. One of the men, still wearing a mask, came in. Suddenly she recalled something she'd noticed last night, his pointed, pixie ears which the mask didn't cover.

'So you're awake at last, Miss Sophie Stone-cum-Stein. I hope you slept well?' he sneered.

'I need the bathroom,' Sophie said coldly.

'There's a chamber pot under the bed,' he replied, and laughed at her look of horror.

Sophie was feeling physically stronger by the minute, and correspondingly angry. 'How the devil am I supposed to manage, tied up like this?'

He sniggered. 'I'll come and help you,

hold you like a babe in arms being potty-trained, I will. I might even wipe your bottom for you if you're nice to me.'

Sophie gritted her teeth, but fortunately the other man appeared in the doorway.

'That's enough!' he snapped. 'You've caused enough trouble! Undo the ropes. The bathroom's along here,' he told Sophie. 'There's no hot water but you'll have the luxury of soap and a towel.'

'Thanks,' she muttered after a pause during which she fought down her anger. He seemed in control, and was at least being civilised. If kidnappers could be called civilised, she amended. It might pay her to keep on as good terms with him as possible.

The younger one—she thought he was younger from his movements and his deference, though sulky, to the other— untied her bonds. It was not accomplished without some unnecessary rubbing against her breasts and thighs, and a hand slipped unnecessarily beneath her skirt, but Sophie bit her lip and endured this. 'My things?' she asked, recalling that they'd made her pack her rucksack, so had presumably brought it with them. 'I'd like to use a toothbrush too, and change into some clean clothes. These have suffered from the floor,' she said, trying to make her tone light rather than complaining.

'It's in the bathroom, but there's nothing you can use to try and escape.'

Sophie stripped off the grubby skirt and blouse and washed. She discovered that they'd removed her small nail scissors and razors, and stuffed everything else back in haphazard fashion. Her watch had been taken from her wrist while she slept. The only remotely sharp item left was the foil-packed strip of throat lozenges she'd bought, and while she despaired of ever being able to cut through the ropes with them she slipped them into her jeans pocket after she'd dressed.

When she was escorted back into the room she found that Luke was awake, still bound but propped against the pillows. He looked dazed, but leaned forward, frowning, when he saw Sophie. 'What the devil?' he began, but the younger man casually slapped him across the mouth and told him to keep his gob shut.

Luke, staggering a little from the drug that had been used on him, was taken to the bathroom. The older man stayed with Sophie.

'If you promise not to cause trouble we'll leave you untied,' he said, to her surprise. 'You can't get out through the window without us hearing, and this is an isolated cottage, and we'd catch you before you got a hundred yards. And there's no one within earshot except the old biddy next door, and she's deaf as a post and practically blind. Besides, if you persuaded her to help you we'd have to eliminate her—like we did dear Gerard. Savvy?'

Sophie nodded slowly. 'What do you want?' she asked. 'Why have you got Luke too?'

'Lover boy? To ensure your good behaviour,' he said, leering.

Sophie shrugged, and sat down on the bed. She was still stiff and exhausted from her night on the floor, and longed to curl up and forget everything. As they didn't appear to be in immediate danger she relaxed. 'I'm so tired,' she said, and yawned.

'Breakfast, then you can sleep on the bed.'

He left her to go downstairs. She wondered whether she could make a dash for it, but Pixie-ears was on the landing, whistling softly under his breath. By the time Luke returned, also in a fresh shirt and jeans, but walking heavily as though he were stiff, the first man had brought a tray with mugs of coffee, and slices of bread spread with jam.

'No fancy food, and you'll have to make do without milk and sugar,' he said curtly. 'Make it last until evening, we don't run to hotel catering.'

They departed, and Sophie heard a bolt being pushed home on the outside of the door. She looked warily at Luke. All this had happened because she hadn't trusted him, had run away from him. She didn't know how, but they must have traced them both because of that. Luke smiled at her however, and nodded towards the food.

'Let's eat, and then talk.'

She found that she was ravenous, and they had soon polished off every last crumb, and drunk the coffee. She was still sleepy, but the stiffness had eased and the intense weariness had dissipated with the wash and the food.

'I'm sorry,' she said quietly. 'Sorry for running away. What happened to you?'

'When I couldn't find you I assumed you'd gone back home, so I went there. They were waiting for me outside, in the lane, and before I knew it I was in their car, trussed and gagged. I've been here for four, or is it five, days? Usually one has been left on guard, while the other's been off every day. Occasionally they trussed me and both went out. Then yesterday they drugged me and that's all I remember until I woke up and found you here. And I've been aching to ask what the devil you've done to your hair.'

Sophie told him briefly how she'd spent the time searching for some news of Rod, and how she'd been helped by Alan Davis. 'I went back to the motel and they were hiding in the bathroom. You were asleep on the bed. I thought you were asleep. Then they injected me with something that knocked me out, and brought me here.'

'Why take me along if they knew you were there? Perhaps they thought I'd manage to escape.'

'Luke, it's all my fault, for not trusting you. I'm sorry!'

He smiled at her, and her heart turned over, but there was a reserve in his eyes that hadn't been there before. 'I think we'd better try and get some rest. I'm shattered, and you must be too. We'll be able to think more clearly when we've slept off the effects of that damned drug.'

They lay down together and pulled the blankets over them. Luke moved very carefully and was scrupulously careful not to touch her, and Sophie longed for him to cradle her in his arms and hold her tight. Soon, though, the softness of the bed enfolded her and she slept.

Judging by the sun it was late afternoon by the time they were woken by Pixie-ears with mugs of tea. He stood outside on the landing, toying with a lethal-looking knife while they each used the bathroom, then leant against the door jamb, leering at them. There were no chairs in the room and they had to sit side by side on the bed.

'Did you have a good screw while you had the chance?' he asked.

'What are you keeping us here for?' Sophie demanded furiously, despite Luke's signal to keep quiet.

'You'll find out soon enough,' he jeered, as he collected the mugs to take downstairs.

'They're even plastic mugs, no use at all

in a fight if it came to that,' Luke said ruefully.

'They took everything sharp from me,' Sophie added. 'But at least we're not tied up now, so we don't need to plan to saw through ropes.'

'That might not last,' he warned. 'They left me loose most of the time, but tied me up when they both went out.'

'They leave?' Sophie asked eagerly.

'They did once or twice.'

'What do they want?'

'Something from you. They kept me only because they thought I could tell them where you were hiding.'

Her eyes widened suddenly. 'Luke, you're moving stiffly. Did they hurt you?'

He shrugged, then winced slightly, though he tried to hide it. 'Not much.'

'Tell me.' When he didn't reply she leaned over and touched him on the arm. He tensed, but held his body steady. 'What did they do to you?' she asked softly. 'Luke, if it was because of me I have a right to know.'

'Just stiffness,' he said. 'It's from where they man-handled me when they caught me. I didn't come quietly.' He grinned, and for a moment the old smile crinkled the corners of his eyes. 'My arm was strained, and being tied up hasn't helped. It's getting better.'

She eyed him doubtfully but he returned her gaze with a bland smile. 'OK. But what can I give them? If they kill me, and it's Rod who's behind it, he'll get all my father's money anyway.'

'You have what your mother and step-father left, Crispins, and your aunt's flat. That must amount to a tidy sum. Have you made a will?'

Sophie shrugged. 'It probably doubles what I'll get from Dad.'

'You left that to your cousin, you said. Where does she live, and does she know?'

'I don't see how she could. She must be about thirty now, and she's a teacher, I think, but I haven't seen her since I was about ten. She used to live somewhere in the north, Cumbria, I think.'

'Why did you name her instead of your brothers?'

'They had enough. It came from her family, not their father. It seemed fairer that she should get it.'

'And she doesn't know. What's her name? I can't go on calling her she.'

'Mary Francis. Unless she's married, but

surely she'd have told me if she had. But she can't know.'

Luke was frowning. 'Then it must be to do with Rod. Let's go through it again. We might spot something. Tell me everything you can about his family.'

She knitted her brows in concentration. 'I told you Dad was married three times. His first wife was Arlene, and they had Rod. He's three years older than me, twenty-five. He works in a New York bank, and has an apartment there. When they got divorced Arlene married Tony Ross. He was divorced too, and I don't know anything about his first wife except that I think she was Italian. Tony's parents had emigrated to the States when he was young, or maybe before he was born. I think originally his name was Rossi. I never took much notice. He and Arlene have a son and a daughter. That's about all I know.'

'Where do they live?'

'In New York usually, but Tony has just gone to work in Belgium, at SHAPE. Arlene was just getting ready to follow when I spoke to her, a couple of days ago.'

Luke was about to speak again when he

paused. Sophie could hear the footsteps on the stairs. 'Later,' Luke said quietly. 'Don't tell them anything.'

The bolt was nosily withdrawn and both their captors came into the room. They still wore their masks, and carried two small wooden chairs which they set down facing Sophie and Luke, who sat side by side on the bed. Pixie-ears smiled, but even though she could see only his eyes, Sophie felt it was more evil than anything else she had ever encountered. His companion carried a small document case which he proceeded to open with slow deliberation. He withdrew a sheaf of papers and then looked up at Sophie. 'I trust you're going to be sensible, my dear.'

She took a deep breath. 'That depends on what you mean by sensible.'

He smiled, mirthlessly. 'You'll be sensible,' he said confidently.

Sophie shot a quick look at Luke, but he was looking down at his hands, clasped loosely together.

'What do you want?'

'Just your name on a piece of paper,' he replied quietly.

'My name? On what piece of paper?'

'You are a very wealthy young woman. It doesn't seem fair that you should benefit, without doing anything to merit such fortune, while others have to struggle just to survive.'

'So? What do you want me to do about it? Give a couple of pence to every single charity in the world? I don't have a lot of cash until I'm twenty-five.'

He laughed, genuinely amused. 'Just one charity,' he said, waving the papers in front of her. 'One will be enough.'

'I wish you'd explain instead of being so silly!' Sophie said in exasperation. Anger was beginning to replace fear, they were being so melodramatic about it.

He frowned, showing the first sign of impatience. 'Very well. This is a paper to gift all your possessions apart from the stables but including the money from your father's books and anything you will inherit from your brother Gerard to your half-brother Rod.'

'Is that all?' Sophie was scornful. 'You're being very abstemious! Don't you want them too?'

'We don't want to leave you without the means of making a living,' he said sharply. 'If you do as we ask you'll stay alive. So will your friend here.'

'Then why have you been trying to kill me? I can understand kidnapping, but being pushed under a train or a motorbike wouldn't do you or Rod any good—he'd only get what my father left then.'

'I have no idea what you're talking about,' he said roughly, but Sophie saw his angry glance at Pixie-ears. 'We've no intention of killing you. Now are you going to sign without any more fuss?'

'No.' Sophie rose to her feet and strode across to the window. As she'd already discovered, there was no help to be had out there. There were no other buildings visible, and beyond a small field a dense, thick wood, almost impenetrable enough to be an enchanted forest, stretched as far as she'd been able to see. 'I won't be bullied into giving away what's mine.'

'I think you will.'

'I'll just repudiate it immediately you let me go, say I was forced into it, so what's the point?' she asked, turning round to face him, genuinely puzzled.

'No. We'll keep your friend until you've been to your solicitor and signed a separate deed of gift. Then you won't be able to dodge your word. And we can always get

263

you at any time, and then most of it will go to Rod anyway.'

Sophie shivered. Suddenly he seemed more menacing than Pixie-ears, who'd remained silent throughout this exchange, though smirking at them unpleasantly.

'I wouldn't trust you. You'd have to kill me anyway, since I could tell people about being forced to sign, and you'd never be safe.'

'Stop poncing about!' He suddenly snarled. 'Despard, take off your shirt!'

Luke sat still, as though he hadn't heard. The boss, as Sophie now thought of him, jerked his head at Pixie-ears, who jumped up and left the room. Within ten seconds he was back, brandishing a short but vicious-looking whip. 'Despard, get ready.'

'No! What are you going to do?' Sophie demanded.

'You'll see. Despard, take off your shirt or we'll take off your pants. Which do you prefer?'

'Luke?' Sophie whispered, and moved towards him. He smiled at her and shook his head.

'Stay away, Sophie. Don't look.'

Pixie-ears grabbed at Luke's shirt and

slowly, painfully, Luke pulled it up over his head. Sophie gasped in horror. Several blood-encrusted weals crisscrossed his back. Now she knew why he'd been moving so stiffly.

'When did they do this to you?' she whispered.

'A few days ago. They're experts in slow torture, a little bit every day.'

Sophie whirled round to face the boss. 'You're inhuman! What has Luke to do with my money? How can beating him help you to steal it? I don't believe you're working for Rod, he'd never agree to this!'

The boss stood up and took the whip from the other. He swished it against the air, and Sophie winced. 'We tried to make the stubborn fool tell us where you were,' he said in a bored voice.

'But he didn't know!'

'Didn't he? How do you think we found you then? Mind you, it was tough. My arm was aching when I'd finished persuading him.'

Sophie pressed her lips together. How had Luke known? How could he have known where she was? Someone had, though. But he'd clearly not betrayed her without immense pressure being brought. She looked at the red, raised stripes on his back again and her own flesh crawled as she imagined the pain he must have suffered.

'Rod ordered it,' the man went on. 'OK, Despard, enough chat. Bend over!'

Sophie clung to his arm as he raised it, but Pixie-ears, with a growl of excited anticipation, pounced on her and flung his arms round her waist. He swung her away and pushed her into a corner of the room just as the first swish of the whip descended on Luke's shoulders. Pixie-ears chuckled, swung Sophie round so that she was facing Luke, and began deliberately fondling her breasts as he held her pinned in front of him. She tried to stamp on his feet, and dig her elbows into his body, but he just laughed while his partner once more brought the whip down on Luke's bare back.

Sophie renewed her struggles, and because her assailant had relaxed his grip as he reached with one hand for her groin, she was able to twist round and claw at his eyes. She managed to pull his mask down and get a brief glimpse of his face, snarling in an animal frenzy, before he punched her in the stomach and she fell backwards against the bed.

He came for her, and she kicked out furiously, then as he backed she levered herself to her feet clutching at the iron bedframe. She kicked again, timing it perfectly and catching him in the crotch. He gave a yelp of pained surprise, and backed away, bent double and clutching at himself.

'You'll pay for that, you dirty bitch!' he gasped. 'Next time it'll be you, not him, and it won't stop with a thrashing! There are better ways of persuading you!'

'Serve you right for pawing her,' the boss said. Then he turned to where Sophie faced him defiantly. 'That's just a taster of what you can expect if you don't sign,' he said coldly.

They went from the room and Sophie turned back to Luke. He was holding the footrail of the bed, his muscles standing out in knots. She picked up his shirt from the floor and stepped towards him.

'You're bleeding,' she said softly. 'Those devils! That's what they've been doing to you for days, isn't it?'

He smiled. It was an effort, more of a grimace than a smile, but Sophie wanted more than anything else in the world to take him in her arms and comfort him.

'I couldn't tell them what I didn't know,' he said gently. 'I didn't know where you were, Sophie, it wasn't through me that they found you.'

'If they'd beaten me like that I'd have said whatever they wanted,' she replied swiftly. 'There's no water to bathe your cuts. Do you want the shirt on? Would it stick to the blood?'

'I'll wait till the bleeding stops,' he said. 'It never lasts very long, I heal quickly.'

She took his hand in her own and stroked it gently. 'You're cold. Lie down on your face, and I'll pile pillows at each side, make a sort of hospital cage so that the sheet doesn't touch your back. At least that will be some warmth.'

He agreed, and when she'd arranged the sheet to her satisfaction Luke began to talk again. 'How did they know you were at that motel? Who else knew?'

Sophie sighed. 'I'm afraid it points to Rod. This university lecturer I met, Alan, phoned Rod and told him where I was, that I wanted to get in touch with him.

He didn't know not to, of course, because I hadn't told him what it was all about. But Rod could have told this pair.'

Luke nodded. 'That sounds a possibility.'

'Who are they? Luke, while we were struggling I pulled down his mask, and I'm sure he's the one who chased me in the Volvo. I caught a glimpse of his face then when you took off his mask, and he has odd shaped ears. I'm certain he's the same man.'

'I'd noticed the ears, and I'm sure you're right. They could be working for Rod. Let's go over again what we know.'

Before they could do so, however, their captors returned. The boss held a sawn-off shotgun, and he trained it on them while the other approached with several lengths of thick twine.

'We're treating ourselves to a good meal, after the exercise this afternoon,' the boss chuckled. 'You can go hungry. And when we've recouped our strength we'll see whether you are more amenable.'

Pixie-ears tied up Sophie first, her hands and then her feet, and made her stand at the end of the bed while he turned to Luke.

'Please don't hurt his back,' she begged impulsively.

'What will you give me then?' he asked suggestively. 'Will you behave yourself, do exactly as I ask?'

'Yes,' she said recklessly.

He guffawed, and tied Luke's feet together, tossing off the sheet she'd so carefully arranged. Then he tied Luke's hands to the iron bars of the bed, pulling his wrists so far through the gaps that Luke had to twist his head awkwardly to avoid being pressed hard against them. Satisfied that the rope was secure he thrust Sophie towards the bed. She collapsed onto it, and found herself sliding as she fell onto the piled-up pillows beside Luke. She thumped painfully to the floor, and heard them laughing as they slammed the door and shot home the bolt. Cramped, lying in an excruciating position, she thought of what she might have to face on the following day, and had difficulty in biting back her tears. But she wouldn't give those brutes the satisfaction of knowing they'd brought her so low. Whatever was in store for her she'd do her utmost not to give way to weak, useless tears.

Chapter Twelve

'Luke, are you OK?' she asked when she'd got her breath back and wriggled into a somewhat less uncomfortable position. He grunted and she was afraid he was in pain.

'Hang on a sec,' he said, and Sophie felt an hysterical desire to giggle. She could hardly move. She wasn't going away. Luke grunted again, and then chuckled. Sophie wondered whether he'd finally flipped, whether the pain and discomfort had got to him so much that he was incapable of rational thought. 'There, that's it,' he muttered.

'What is?' she asked. 'Luke, what's going on?'

'I hadn't noticed before, no reason to investigate the back of the bed, but there's a rough edge just where they've tied my hands. I might be able to saw through the twine. It's not very thick.'

Sophie was silent, listening to the constant rasping noise as Luke rubbed the twine which bound his hands up and down against the metal. Once or twice he stifled a groan, and Sophie tried to count the minutes. Their tormentors would, she reckoned, be away for at least an hour, but they couldn't depend on much more. She had no way of telling the time, she'd heard no clocks chiming or church bells ringing. She tried counting in seconds but after about ten minutes lost count and gave up. It didn't matter. Either Luke would get free and they'd have a chance of escape or he wouldn't, and she'd have to face that rotten little beast and endure whatever he subjected her to. On one thing, she was determined: Luke should not have to go through more whipping if she could prevent it.

To distract herself she began to go through everything that had happened, trying to find the slightest bit of information she might have forgotten, which would be of help. Her arms were stiff, numb where she was lying awkwardly, and she realised that unless she kept supple she might delay them by being unable to move once Luke got free and released her. She began to wriggle her toes and hands, and gradually managed to roll over and push herself into a sitting position against the wardrobe. It was better, she could flex her legs and her arms, and it mattered less that her bottom was getting numb from the unyielding floorboards.

It seemed like hours later that Luke's occasional grunt gave way to a crow of triumph. He had freed his hands, and he rolled over and sat up stiffly. His fingers were clumsy, but he was able to unknot the twine that bound his legs, and then he knelt down to release Sophie. He dropped a swift kiss on her nose, and helped her to stand.

'Which way? Can we break down the door?' she asked.

'The window will be better. It's not a big drop, and we can go in the traditional way with the sheets.'

Sophie laughed. 'The windows are painted shut,' she pointed out.

'No matter, they left a chair which will be perfect for breaking the glass. Thank goodness they're large panes.'

As he spoke he shoved the chest aside, seized the chair and began to attack the window.

'Get our clothes together, we may as well take them,' he said. 'We can dump them if we're chased, but they'll come in handy if we have to sleep out tonight.'

Sophie stuffed the clothes that were lying about into her rucksack, added her shoulderbag and pulled on an extra sweater and her anorak. She sorted out a shirt and sweater from Luke's clothes, and pushed the rest into the tote bag he'd been using.

'Get dressed, I'll do that,' she ordered as he pushed the chair aside and began to knot the two sheets together. She folded a blanket and placed it over the jagged edges of glass, then looked out. There was a water butt beneath the window, and the drop to it was no more than three metres at most.

'Help me drag the bed,' Luke gasped, and she seized one end and they pulled it as close to the window as possible. Luke tied one end of the sheets round the bars, while Sophie threw out their belongings. There was no time to lower them gently to the ground. 'You first. Shall I tie you?'

'Waste of time,' Sophie said, panting from her exertions. She clambered over the bed and went backwards, inelegant but fast, through the window. For a moment she swung wildly, and prayed the sheets

274

would hold, then her foot connected with the water butt and she managed to keep her balance and jump to the ground. By the time she looked upwards Luke was coming down after her.

'Come on, as far as we can as fast as we can,' he ordered, and grabbing his tote bag set off towards the fence which separated the small garden from the field. Sophie slung her rucksack over her shoulder, gasped as her arms protested, and followed.

They reached the shelter of the trees just as a car's headlights swung across the front of the house, and threw themselves down under some tangled undergrowth. They watched, and breathed a sigh of relief as the car went on.

'Come on, into the trees, and I suspect we'll have to wait till morning to find our way out again,' Luke said, laughing.

'I don't care, and I'm going to walk all night,' Sophie declared. She glanced upwards. 'There's a full moon, we can see by that and steer by the stars.'

Half an hour later she was beginning to regret her words. Her legs ached, felt heavier with every step, and she was certain she had at least a ton of mud on each shoe, they were so enormous and difficult to move each step of the way.

As they crossed a small clearing she glanced at Luke. He was gripping his lip with his teeth, and Sophie knew he must be suffering even worse than she was. There had been no time to deal with the cuts on his back, and the touch of the shirt, let alone the sweater he was wearing, must be agony.

'Let's take a break,' she said abruptly. 'I don't think I can go on for another minute without a rest.'

'We ought to get as far away as possible,' Luke said. 'Even if we've walked in a straight line we can't be more than a mile from the house.'

'They'll have trouble finding us, and this time we're free, we can fight. Plenty of cudgels around,' she added, looking at the many fallen branches. It was an old wood. The tracks they had been following were overgrown, and often seemed no more than deer tracks. 'Besides, we'll feel more able to fight if we have to after we've had a rest. There's no point in getting so exhausted we'd just give in.'

Luke sighed and looked round. 'Let's

get off the path then. There's some thick undergrowth over in that direction. We'll burrow into that and take it in turns to snooze.'

When they had found a space in the middle of a tangle of bushes, soft with fallen leaves and pine needles, Sophie insisted on taking the first watch. 'I slept this afternoon, but you were beaten up,' she said. 'Have you another sweater to put on? Use the rucksack for a pillow.'

'You're going to make somebody a very bossy wife,' he murmured as he stretched out on his stomach, eased his shoulders, put his head onto the rucksack and fell straight asleep.

Sophie looked at him, pale in the moonlight and his face dappled with the tracery of leaves and branches above them. She could still see the firmness of his jaw, the slightly crooked nose which was only visible from certain angles, the contrast of the fair hair, long and flopping over eyes which she knew were such a dark brown they were almost black, and the clearly defined lips. She desperately wanted to touch those lips, to trace their shape with her fingers. She wondered whether she'd feel them on her own once more. After all he'd gone through on her behalf he'd probably never want to see her again.

That thought banished the euphoria she'd been feeling since they'd made their escape. Having got free of their kidnappers once didn't mean they were safe. They could get her any time at Crispins. And no doubt they knew where Luke lived too. They'd have searched him, found his address or a card or driving licence. He wouldn't be safe unless they could put the men in prison. But she had no idea who they could be, where to find them again. The house hadn't seemed like someone's home from what she'd seen of it. It was more like a cheap rented place. If they'd rented it they would have done so with false names, paid cash, probably never seen the agent. When they found the prison empty they'd leave, go to ground, find another base with the advantage of knowing where their quarry could be found.

Had Rod sent them? Sophie found it difficult to believe. He had plenty of money, he didn't need hers and Gerard's too. Yet who else would benefit?

She worried at it until she noticed a faint lightening of the sky. Luke hadn't moved, and she'd been chary of waking him. With his cuts and bruises he needed to rest, and she could do without sleep for a while. She'd sat up many nights with sick horses or mares giving birth. As soon as it was light enough to see, though, they ought to move, put a greater distance between themselves and the house. If they could find a road they could perhaps hitch a lift to the nearest town and then decide what to do, where to go.

Luke stirred and gave an involuntary moan. Gradually he eased himself into a sitting position and cautiously stretched his arms.

'It's almost daylight,' he said accusingly. 'Why didn't you wake me?'

'I wasn't sleepy,' Sophie said, 'and you needed to rest. How do you feel?'

'Hungry and thirsty,' he said. 'We'd better find a road or a farmhouse soon. Luckily they didn't take my wallet.'

'All I have are some throat lozenges,' Sophie said and offered him one. 'They won't be very sustaining, but it's something to suck.'

They set off straight away. Sophie's physical weariness had eased, but it seemed a long time before they found the edge of the wood. By now it was full daylight and they could hear some farm machinery in the distance. The wood petered out in a straggle of saplings, and a narrow, twisting road which ran alongside.

'It can't be very busy,' Sophie said, indicating the dozens of pheasants along the grass verge, in the woods, the fields opposite, even on the roadway.

They'd been too preoccupied to discuss what they meant to do once they reached civilisation, now they looked at one another and smiled. 'How's your back?' Sophie asked.

'Better than I thought when I woke up,' Luke said. 'Activity seems beneficial. In all that exertion last night I scarcely felt the cuts.'

'It was my fault, for not trusting you,' Sophie said remorsefully.

'We might just as easily have gone back to Crispins and both of us been caught,' he pointed out.

'Yes, but then they wouldn't have beaten you up for information you didn't have.'

'Look, that's past. We have to decide what to do now.'

'Walk, until we can hitch a lift or get a bus,' she said. 'Which way?'

'East,' he decided. 'They won't have

gone nearer to London, and it's too isolated here.'

'It feels like Wychwood Forest,' Sophie said thoughtfully. 'That's the biggest area of woodland anywhere near Oxford, and unless we've been wandering round and round in a smaller area or were taken much further away it's a possible place. In that case Oxford's to the east.'

'Let's find out.'

They walked for a couple of miles, diving into the hedge or ditch every time they heard a car. Then they heard a heavier vehicle coming and after a quick consultation decided to chance trying to get a lift. They stood looking hopeful, and the driver of a flatbed lorry brought it squealing to a halt.

'We're heading for Oxford,' Luke said. 'Can you help?'

'As far as the bypass. Hop up.'

Sophie went first, and they discovered that it was ten miles or so to Oxford.

'You're out early,' their driver said. 'Most hitchers don't get started till later, unless they've been travelling overnight.'

'Yes, we were,' Luke said.

'From the university?'

'Just visiting. Are you going far?' he

asked, anxious to deflect further questions.

'Ten miles further on, towards North-ampton. I'll drop you at the Peartree roundabout. Know your way from there? You can get a meal and a wash if you want, and then a bus into the centre.'

'Yes,' Sophie said in a small voice. She wasn't at all sure she wanted to be back at the scene of her abduction.

It seemed a very short time before he pulled onto the verge and they thanked him profusely for the ride. They stood and waved as he drove off, then spent a considerable time negotiating the wide roads which led to the flyover, and were busy with early morning traffic.

'A coffee?' Luke suggested.

'Isn't it too dangerous? Won't they be looking for us here?'

'They aren't going to suspect we've come here. It's probably the last place they'll look. And there's not much they can do in a big busy cafe. They can scarcely wear masks, and they'd be worried we could recognise them.'

'You've convinced me! Breakfast too, everything. We didn't have any lunch yesterday or dinner last night.'

By the time they'd eaten and stocked

up with bars of chocolate from the shop Sophie felt much better.

'What now? The police?' Luke asked as they emerged from the cafe.

Sophie was about to nod and then paused. 'They want us for Gerard's death,' she recalled. 'Pru said they'd eliminated everyone else.' She'd almost forgotten that she was suspected of that, and in running away had confirmed the police's suspicions.

'We'd be safe in prison, while they sort it out,' Luke said, grinning.

'Maybe, but there are things I need to do. I want to go and see Alan Davis,' she said. 'I have a lot of questions to ask, and he would let us have a bath, which both of us need. I could put some ointment on those cuts.'

'In the bath?' Luke asked, and Sophie blushed scarlet. She was reminded of the time he'd seen her in the bath.

'I'll ask Alan to do it.'

'Pity. I haven't met him, but somehow I doubt he's as attractive as you.'

Sophie began to walk away. 'Come on, it's a ten minute walk.'

He grinned and followed. 'Yes, ma'am. As I said, some poor devil's going to have

283

an uncomfortable life with you.'

She glared at him and he seized her hand, holding it tightly as she tried to pull away. 'Let go,' she snapped.

'Sophie, wait a moment. Do you trust this Alan chap? You didn't know him, did you, before he picked you up in Oxford?'

'He didn't pick me up!'

'Look, don't get mad at me. He knows Rod, he's admitted that. You've no proof he's what he says he is. He might be part of the conspiracy, have been watching you in Oxford, looking for a chance to gain your confidence.'

'This gets more and more impossible! And I do have proof, at least that he was a tutor on the course, because he took me to see two of the others. You're not going to suggest there's a whole gang of them setting themselves up in Oxford flats just to bamboozle me, are you?'

'It does sound unlikely. OK, let's go and wring the professor dry of all he knows. But Sophie, let's be careful what we tell him, just in case he accidentally passes it on. It was probably his message to Rod that enabled those crooks to find you.'

To Sophie's secret relief Alan answered the

door at once. He was carrying a bowl in his hand, and milk from his cornflakes was dripping over the edge.

'Sophie! Where have you been? I've been worried sick. When I went round to the motel the next day the police were there. The window of your room had been broken and they thought someone had got in from the balcony.' That explained the draught, they must have climbed up that way, then fetched Luke from their car, Sophie thought. Alan was still speaking. 'No one knew where you'd gone. Your clothes had all gone, but there were pyjamas under the pillow. They've been searching for you. Oh, come in, I beg your pardon.'

He ushered them into the room and looked round for an empty space to put down his cornflakes and eventually balanced them on top of a pile of folders.

'This is Luke, a friend,' Sophie said briskly. 'Alan, did Rod ring back?'

'No, and that's another odd thing. I rang him again, and had so much trouble getting through I went through the operator. They told me the number was no longer in use.'

'What? But how could it?'

Sophie looked at Alan in disbelief. 'Try it,' he offered. 'I meant to try again, but I've been busy with a special course.'

Sophie fished out her address book and they all went into the kitchen. She sat by the telephone and began to dial. She was past caring that it would be the middle of the night in New York. When she had fared no better than Alan she turned back to him. He was pouring out another bowl of cornflakes, and Sophie wondered whether the pot plant, which looked in a better state than on her previous visit, would have the benefit of his abandoned bowl when he eventually found it again.

'Coffee?' Alan offered, and pulled out a jar of instant. As he filled the kettle he spoke over his shoulder. 'By the way, I discovered when Rod went back to the States. Let me look in my diary. Yes, it was Sunday.'

'That was two days before Gerard died,' Sophie said, surprised. By now she was convinced Rod had killed their brother. 'How can you be sure?'

'One of the other students travelled back with him. He hadn't been booked on that flight, but he told this chap there was something urgent he had to do in New York. The man happened to telephone me about some information, some articles he'd promised to send me, and he mentioned it.'

'I'll ring his bank. Oh, it's too early. I wonder if I could contact his mother?'

'Go ahead,' Alan said generously, seemingly oblivious to the mounting cost of his international telephone bill.

Sophie eventually found the Belgium number, spoke to someone at SHAPE, and was eventually connected to Rod's step-father, Tony Ross. She wrote down a number and dialled again. After a considerable time the telephone was answered.

'What is it?'

'Arlene? It's Sophie here. Do you know where Rod is?'

'Asleep, I imagine, as I wish I was. I'm still jet-lagged, days after getting to this lousy place.'

'I can't raise his home number. It's been disconnected. And the last time anyone got through it was answered by a woman. Has he moved?'

'Why shouldn't he have a woman there? He's past the age of consent, honey.'

Sophie put down the receiver. 'She

neither knows nor appears to care. Alan, we've been sleeping rough. Would you be a darling and let us have hot baths? And do you have any ointment for cuts? Luke had an accident, and we haven't been able to see to them.'

'Sure. This way. But what's been happening, Sophie? Why was your room at the motel broken into?'

'Um, I don't know, but nothing was stolen, and I moved somewhere else,' Sophie said. 'I didn't have a chance to let you know, so much was happening.' It was the literal truth, so long as she considered herself as nothing. She'd been stolen, all right, but Alan didn't need to know. She hadn't believed Luke's suggestion that he might be in league with Rod, but it was highly likely that Rod had discovered where she was through Alan.

'Use the back room, it's the spare, and there isn't room to swing a towel in the bathroom. Plenty of towels in the cupboard on the landing. And there's ointment in the bathroom cupboard. Heavens, is that the time? I'm due at college in twenty minutes. Can I leave you to it? I'll be back in a couple of hours, and I'll bring in something for lunch.'

'Trusting chap,' Luke commented as the front door slammed.

'You go first, and then I'll put the ointment on.'

She sat on the spare bed as she waited, trying to work it out. Rod had left before he could have killed Gerard. But hadn't someone said his brother had visited him the day before he died? Who was that if it wasn't Rod? Could he have come straight back? If so why had he gone in the first place? Then there were the supposed cousins. How could she discover the likely names of the couple who had visited him? Perhaps Karen would know, and by now be calmer and able to talk. She'd telephone her when she'd had her bath.

Luke came in, wearing jeans. Sophie closed her eyes to shut out the sight of his lacerated, bruised back.

'Oh, Luke! You poor darling! Let me spread this ointment.'

He submitted, and she smoothed the ointment over the cuts. None of them, she was thankful to see, looked puffy or septic, and on close examination there were fewer actual skin breakages than had at first appeared.

'It might still be a good idea to see a

doctor, though,' she said as she screwed the top on the tube of ointment.

'How would I explain it? And it's just sore, I'll mend. Now go and have your bath. Luckily there seems to be plenty of hot water.'

Sophie was thankful to change into clean clothes. They were her last underclothes and tee shirt, and both pairs of jeans were so disreputable she had to wear the track suit. When she went downstairs Luke had made real coffee, and she sat in the kitchen, almost falling asleep.

'I'd better try Rod's bank,' she said at last. 'No, I'll try Gerard's mother first.'

There was no reply, so she tried his step-father's office, to be told that Herr Hoffmann was still on compassionate leave, they believed somewhere in England. She eventually got through to someone at Rod's bank, who said there was no one higher up there yet, but as far as she knew Rod Stein no longer worked for them.

'What in the world's going on? Rod seems to have disappeared completely! He's left his job, had his phone cut off, and yet he couldn't have killed Gerard.'

'Could he have been kidnapped too?' Luke asked.

'But what would be the point? They wanted me to sign everything over to him.'

'If he has it, from you and Gerard, and then he dies, who would get it then? Your father made provision for one of you, even two, dying, but he could never have envisaged all three of you dying so young.'

Sophie was staring at him. 'He could leave it how he wanted. If I'd had any brothers or sisters, from Mom's second marriage, I'd have left it to them,' she said slowly. 'Surely, even if someone dies without making a will, their closest relatives normally benefit.'

'And Rod has a brother and sister. Tell me about them.'

'Rita's a year or so younger than I am, Ben's a bit older. They're both at colleges in America. Ben's studying medicine, Rita's doing some kind of art course, history of art, I think.'

'Medicine. Drugs. The knowledge to kill Gerard and drugs to put us out for the count.'

'But I can't believe Ben would try to murder Gerard! Nor Rita.'

'Didn't you say once that Arlene's new

husband had children by a first marriage? They'd be older.'

Sophie shivered. 'And I don't know where they are. I've never even seen them. I'm sure they have Italian names, though, Guido and Riccardo, I think. Yes, I've heard Rod mention Ricky.'

'Those two didn't have Italian accents, nor American. They were slightly East End.'

'Their mother came back to Europe, I believe. I'd assumed it was to Italy, but it could have been to London,' Luke said slowly. 'And they'd only have been three and four or so when that happened.'

'And if Ben's involved too, they'd need all my money to share, or they are especially greedy. I'm going to phone Pru. She may know something. Karen might be there. And it might have been them, or one of them and a woman, who visited Gerard in hospital, the couple I don't know.'

'The police had eliminated them.'

'It was only Pru who said that. The police suspect me! They can make mistakes.'

She began to dial. After a minute Mrs Miller answered. 'Mrs Miller, it's Sophie. I need to speak to Pru. Is she there?'

'Miss Sophie! Oh, my stars! Where've

you been all this while? You've had us all that worried! Why didn't you phone and let us know you were all right?'

'I'm phoning now,' Sophie said as patiently as she could. 'Please can you get Pru? I need to speak to her urgently, and I haven't much time.'

'I'll see if she's in the garden. She may be with her boyfriend. Ever so excited she was, when he turned up unexpectedly this morning. Just back from some foreign place, she said.'

It was a couple of minutes before Pru, sounding breathless, spoke. 'Sophie! We've been worried sick! Where are you?'

'In Oxford. Is Karen there?'

'No, they wouldn't stay here, they're at some posh hotel in Marlow, I think. Sophie, are you coming home?'

'With the police wanting me? Do you have the faintest idea which hotel?'

'Sorry, no. But the police don't want you. They've decided that it was an accident after all. Look, shall I come and fetch you? Is Luke with you? Did he find you? He was in a terrible state when he left here.'

Sophie looked at the phone in her hand. 'No, thanks, Pru. I can get home myself.'

She replaced the receiver and turned

to Luke. 'That's odd. When you went back to Crispins, when did those men ambush you?'

'Before I got there,' he said.

'Yes, I thought that was what you said.'

Chapter Thirteen

'There are some questions I need to ask Pru. And Karen, but she's at some hotel in Marlow. I think we'd better tell Karen. She can't be involved.'

'Let's hire a car, try Marlow. Where's she likely to be staying? Shall we try phoning round first?' Luke offered.

'Karen only stays at the very best hotels. I bet you it'll be the Compleat Angler,' Sophie said with a slight laugh. 'She's fussy because she doesn't like hotels. I'm curious that she'd go there. Especially now, when she could stay at Crispins.'

'Perhaps it's because you weren't at home.'

'Maybe.' Sophie didn't sound convinced. 'I'd rather surprise her. Pru says the police think it's an accident, they don't suspect me, but Karen may be suspicious.'

'Let's find a rental car.'

By the time they had that organised Alan was back, carrying a veritable feast from an Indian takeaway. An hour later they were on the road to Marlow.

As they went under the wide, low arch towards the hotel entrance of The Compleat Angler they almost collided with Franz Hoffman on his way out. 'Sophie, good afternoon,' he said gravely. 'Have you come to see us? Karen is upstairs in our room.'

'How is she? Have the police discovered any more?'

'They do not say, and it makes her very unsettled. But where have you been all this time? She has been very worried for you, and the police are still wanting to talk to you.'

'The police have decided it wasn't an accident?'

'It seems so. They are still asking questions, they are treating it as murder still.'

'Can I see her, and I'll explain.'

He led the way through the hotel and up to their room, where Karen was sitting by the window, staring out at the river, the sound of the weir coming through the open window. She looked round, then rose to meet Sophie.

'Child, where have you been?' she asked, coming to hug her.

Sophie explained the odd attacks which had been made on her, and her fear that it was someone out to get both of them, her and Gerard.

'Plus the police were suspecting me, and so I went into hiding from the police and whoever it was trying to murder us all.'

'Rod,' Franz said heavily.

'Or someone working with him. He went back to America two days before Gerard was killed, so he wasn't directly involved, and he couldn't have attacked me. He's not at the bank so far as I can discover, and his telephone's been cut off. He wouldn't do such suspicious things if he wanted to establish some alibi, pretend to be uninvolved.' She glanced at Luke. 'Besides, Luke and I have been kidnapped. We only got away this morning.'

Karen exclaimed and wanted to know all the details. Franz was frowning as they told her some of them.

'So someone wants all the money, and

it seems that Rod, if he's not behind it, will be in danger once he's inherited it,' Franz said thoughtfully.

'Yes. Which leaves his family. Unless these crooks try to force Rod to sign it over to them. Do you know anything about Tony Ross's two older sons, by his first wife? Where are they?'

'They were brought up in England. I believe their mother remarried, and they may even have taken her husband's name,' Franz said slowly.

'That fits. These men were about the right ages, they looked rather alike in colouring and general build, although we never saw their faces. And a man and a woman we can't trace visited Gerard on the last day. Plus Rod's half-brother Ben is a medical student, he'd be able to get the drugs which knocked us out. Either Rod's involved or he's going to be in danger, the same as I am. I'm going home to talk to Pru, and then I'll call the police.'

'We'll follow. I was just going out to see the undertaker about arrangements for taking Gerard's body home. The inquest was adjourned again and the police have released his body,' he said quietly. 'We'll be half an hour or so behind you.'

They crossed the bridge back into the town and Luke concentrated on weaving through the busy high street. Sophie was thinking hard.

'What do you want to ask Pru?' Luke said, as they were driving up the dual carriageway towards High Wycombe.

'She said, when you went there looking for me, that you were distraught. But you said you were jumped before you got there.'

'I didn't see Pru.'

'And she said the police were not still looking for me, suspecting me, but Franz thinks they are.'

They drove in silence as Luke negotiated the busy Handy Cross roundabout. As he braked going down the steep hill into the town Sophie shuddered.

'It was here they got Gerard. That wall alongside's where he must have hit his head.'

Luke put his hand over hers briefly, and they didn't speak again until they'd got through the town and were climbing out on the far side of the narrow valley. Then she had to direct him through the tangle of lanes where they'd first met. Luke kept glancing in the rear view mirror, and eventually Sophie twisted round to see what was happening.

'What is it?'

'That car's been behind us for a long time.'

She tried to see the driver's face, but the car was too far away. Several times it could have turned off, but it stayed behind them. Then, on the same straight stretch where Sophie had been so terrorised before it speeded up. As Sophie watched she was flung against the seat belt when Luke braked hard and the car went into a skid.

'Get out, into the trees, hide!' Luke shouted as the car juddered to a halt against the verge, and Sophie, blindly obeying, caught a glimpse of another car drawn full across the road in front of them, and a masked man holding a gun stepping out.

Sophie clambered up the bank and sped away, Luke a few steps behind her. There was a rough track in front, like that other, and similarly blocked by a huge log. They vaulted the log together and hurtled along the track, round a bend which took them out of sight of the road, and suddenly dipped down the side of a steep hill.

Luke grabbed Sophie's hand and pulled her amongst the trees. She glanced at him and nodded, and quietly now, taking care to keep well away from the track, they threaded their way through the wood.

They could hear the pursuit as the men raced along the track. Then it grew fainter and Sophie relaxed.

'Can we get back to the car?' she asked.

Luke shook his head. 'Best not to. They were blocking the road both ways, and there are probably a few other people up there by now, furious at the delay and blocking it even more. When we rode over here it was about three miles, I think? We'll walk.'

'I can find the way without using the paths, then if they get close we can hide. Luckily this isn't only a beech wood, so there's plenty of undergrowth.'

They'd covered about a mile, she estimated, down into one narrow valley and up to the opposite ridge, when they had to leave the shelter of the trees and cross an open ploughed field which sloped down towards another of the deep narrow valleys which were typical of the Chilterns. Beyond it was a lane, following the valley floor, and another field full of cattle, sloping steeply towards a different, conifer planted wood. In the distance they could hear a tractor, but it wasn't in sight. They were just across the lane and scrambling over a stile when a car came hurtling along, and screeched to a halt. The door opened, and one of their pursuers stepped out.

They took to their heels, but it was heavy going up the slope, and the cattle, scared of all this activity, blundered about getting in their way. Then there was a shot, and the cattle stampeded. Sophie was nudged aside by one panic-stricken heifer, thrown heavily against Luke who clasped her to his chest as he struggled to stay on his feet.

'To the hedge,' he gasped, and took her hand and dragged her to the nearest one. As they threw themselves down and scrabbled through holes at the base another shot sounded, close behind them.

Sophie heard the pellets skitter through the leaves above them, and felt an irrational sense of relief. Nasty as pellet wounds could be, especially at close range, it seemed as though their pursuers didn't intend to kill them at once. Then, her shirt torn by the thorns above, and her knees bruised by the sharp flints below, she was through the hedge and picked herself up. This field was ploughed, either already sown with a winter crop, or ready for it. The furrows were parallel to the hedge, which helped as they struggled on towards the trees. She could hear the frightened lowing of the cattle as they huddled at the far end of their field, but also the panting of the man stalking them.

Luke took her hand. 'There's only one,' he whispered in her ear, breathing heavily from the exertion. 'They had two cars, and must have split up to quarter the roads. Let's tackle him.'

'How?' Sophie demanded. 'And what are you doing?' Luke was bending every few steps to pick up the flints which had been thrown up by the plough.

'When we get to the trees you go on, making a noise, and when he follows I'll be behind him. I'm quite handy with stones, and I can probably find a fallen branch too. Anyway, I'll jump him. Have you anything on you we can tie him up with?'

'Socks?' she gasped.

'He might have a belt. We'll manage, till we can get him back to the car. I'll knock him out if necessary, but he'll be a weight to carry. Get ready to let me have your socks as soon as I've got him.'

They reached the trees, gaining a few minutes because the pasture had a hedge round it which it took the other man a while to negotiate. They darted inside, and Luke found a thickly branched conifer to hide behind. He squeezed Sophie's hand and she ran on, making more noise than necessary as she zigzagged through the trees. Behind her she heard a shot, heard pellets whistle past her ears, even felt a couple, possibly deflected by the branches above, fall onto her hair. Then there was a shout and the sound of a scuffle, grunts and a sudden yelp of pain. She turned and wove her way back towards Luke, and had almost reached him when he called out to her.

'He's out cold. Come back, Sophie.'

'I think I may have broken his arm,' Luke said ruefully, looking down at the man lying on the ground. He'd removed the mask, and it was Pixie-ears. 'Never mind, he'd have done worse to us. One down and one to go.'

'How did it happen? And even so, oughtn't we to tie him up?' She was already taking off her shoes and socks.

Luke had unbuckled the man's belt and was pulling it through the loops. 'We'd better use both.' He explained as he efficiently bound the man's feet together, 'I used a branch to trip him up, and then got the gun away. It was while we were fighting for that I knelt on his arm and he twisted, and the bone snapped. Then I knocked him out.'

'We can use his car to get home. Do we have to carry him, or could we leave him here while we tell the police?'

'Hallo there! What's going on?' a new voice intervened.

Sophie turned round, alarmed, then sighed with relief. 'It's the man who farms these fields,' she told Luke. 'I know him quite well. Mr King! This man was chasing us, shooting at us,' she explained.

'I was ploughing and heard the noise, and saw that something had upset my beasts, so came to see what was going on. What are you going to do with him?'

'Carry him down to his car and take him back with us, turn him over to the police. There's much more to it.'

He eyed them, amusement in his eyes. 'I'll help you carry him. But you may as well bring him to the house, and we'll phone the police from there. Sophie, lass, you carry the gun.'

'Thanks.'

It was a struggle for the two men, carrying their burden across the ploughed field, especially as he came to and began to struggle when they'd almost reached the farmhouse. Without Mr King they'd have had a much worse task.

They dumped him in a chair in the kitchen, and Mr King, kicking off his muddy boots, went to telephone the police. When he came back Sophie drew him outside, out of Pixie-ears' hearing.

'There's another one, and he knows where I live. I'm afraid for Pru,' she said swiftly. 'I know we shouldn't leave before the police come, but we'll be held up for hours when they do. We need reinforcements if his pal's at the stables. Can you ring again and ask them to meet us there?'

'You ought to stay,' he said doubtfully.

'I know, but if they send one man it's not much help. Ring and tell them there's another one, and he's armed too, and dangerous. Mr King, Pru might be on her own!'

He relented. 'Best go quickly then, before they turn up.'

'Bless you. I'll come and tell you all about it soon.'

They reached Crispins without further adventures. Pru's Mini was near the front door, beside it a Vauxhall Astra.

'Looks as though Karen and Franz got here before us,' Luke said as he parked beside them.

'It doesn't look like a car Franz would hire. The other man might be here,' Sophie said, worried.

They looked round but saw nothing else apart from a builder's lorry near the barn, loaded with timber. Sophie took a deep breath and walked towards the kitchen door, pausing when it opened and Rod appeared on the step.

'Rod!'

'Hello,' he said, glancing in puzzlement at Sophie's hair. 'You look different somehow.'

'Rod, where the devil have you been? We've been trying to call you, but first a woman answered, then your phone's been disconnected, and the bank said you weren't with them any longer.'

'No. Rita was staying there for a while, but now I've rented out my apartment. That's why I came to see you. I'd been ill for several weeks, then I was in Japan the week before I saw you, and I've been offered a two-year contract out there. That's why I was so jet-lagged and incoherent when I saw you, I'd been on planes for almost a week, I think.'

'You said you'd ring me.'

'I meant to, but Gerard seemed to be doing OK, and I had a sudden call from Japan. I had to get back to hand in my notice and clear my desk sooner than I'd expected.'

'Let's go in,' Sophie said.

Pru was sitting in one of the armchairs beside the Aga, and gasped in surprise when she saw Sophie. She struggled to her feet.

'Sophie! Where have you been, and what on earth have you done to your hair?'

Sophie was looking at the man in the other armchair, who'd made no attempt to rise. She had to make a conscious effort to recall him. He was dark haired and deeply tanned, as though he'd just spent a long time at some tropical resort or was of Mediterranean origin. She belatedly recognised Pru's new boyfriend, who'd been helping to train pilots in some Arab sheikdom. She smiled tentatively, unsure whether he'd remembered her, for they'd met so briefly. Then something about his eyes, brown and expressionless, made her pause.

'Guy got here just minutes ago, Sophie!' Pru said, her voice shrill with excitement. 'He's back for a couple of weeks, he was telling me. You don't mind if he stays here, do you? There's plenty of room since Karen took the huff and walked out.'

'Guy. Of course. You're Guido Rossi, aren't you?'

He raised his eyebrows. 'I haven't any idea what you're talking about,' he said languidly, but Sophie wasn't listening. She swung round towards Pru, her eyes wide with shock and distress.

Rod spoke. 'He hasn't been called Guido for years, Sophie, since his mother married an Essex man.'

Sophie was still looking at Pru. 'That's why they didn't want me to give them Crispins. You'd have it anyway. Pru, did you know they were trying to kill me? Were you part of it all along?'

Guy reached down beside his chair, and

as Luke dived towards him he swung the shortened shotgun round. Rod uttered a surprised shout, but Luke was on top of Guy, and as they struggled and Rod moved tentatively towards them Pru tried to push him away.

'No, Rod, it's all right. Keep out of it! Guy can—'

Then the gun went off, the sound deafening inside the room, and Sophie saw rather than heard Pru's cry of shock as she staggered back, clutching her chest. Rod tried to hold her up, but she slid through his grasp and fell to the ground.

'OK, I've got him, get me some rope or twine,' Luke gasped, and Sophie came to with a start and ran to get a ball of nylon string from one of the kitchen drawers.

'Will this do?'

'What's going on?' Rod demanded, looking round from where he was attempting to staunch the bleeding from Pru's chest.

'Until we can get something stronger. Keep still!' Luke added and Sophie went to help, twisting the string tightly round their former captor's wrists.

They hauled him, kicking and swearing, onto a kitchen chair and bound him to that until he was trussed and immobile. Then Sophie rushed across to where Pru lay.

She was crumpled into an untidy heap, her face pale, bleeding profusely from the wound in her chest. That had not been pellets, Sophie knew, as she grabbed cloths and tried to help Rod stem the bleeding.

'I'll phone for an ambulance,' Luke said.

'Where's my brother?' Guy asked, aware that there was no way of bluffing this time.

'With the police, I expect,' Luke said. 'They are on their way here, and I think it sounds as though the reinforcements are arriving now.'

'Police?' Rod asked. 'What police? And what's Guy been doing? Why did he have a gun?'

'He killed Gerard, has been trying to kill me, and when you'd inherited all our money he'd have killed you,' Sophie said briefly. 'Hang on, Pru, they'll be here soon.'

Before Rod could ask anything else the police had entered the room, followed shortly by the ambulance crew.

'I'll go with her,' Sophie insisted, and scrambled into the ambulance.

'Very well, Miss, and we'll take the fellow who shot her, and you,' a policeman added, turning to Luke and Rod, 'can come to the station to give a statement.'

'We'll see you tomorrow, Miss,' the other one told Sophie.

* ★ ★ ★

Sophie knelt beside Pru and clasped her hand as the paramedics worked on her, and the ambulance sped through the winding lanes, siren blaring.

'I didn't mean to harm you,' Pru said, her words faint and jerky.

'Hush, now, it's all right,' Sophie tried to reassure her, but Pru didn't seem able to stop talking.

'I was always jealous of you, when we were children. You had your own pony and I had to work for my rides. Then I married David, and I thought after he died I'd have enough money to do what I wanted. But he took so long to die, it seemed like years waiting to be free of him.'

Sophie stared at her. Surely she wasn't implying that she'd killed her elderly husband? Pru didn't appear to notice Sophie's slight withdrawal.

'I loved you too, Sophie. But you went on getting more and more. I thought if you married John we could all enjoy it, but you wouldn't. When I met Guy it seemed it was meant to happen. We didn't mean to kill anyone, just persuade you. But Gerard got away and was coming to tell you.'

'Gerard?' Sophie exclaimed.

'Guy and Ricky kept him prisoner for a week, tried to persuade him, when he came to England for a holiday. He got away. He must have been hiding for at least a week, then he sent you that card. They didn't dare let you talk to him.'

'They'd been trying to kill me for a couple of months before that!' Sophie said, in her indignation allowing her voice to rise so that the paramedic looked at her disapprovingly.

'Let her be quiet,' he said.

Pru wasn't going to be quiet. 'That was Ricky on his own, trying to kill you. He was too impatient with Guy's plan. They quarrelled dreadfully about it. Then Luke appeared so conveniently. They kept watch on him too, and Ricky tried to get you in London, and blame him, but you were so lucky. You always escaped.'

'How did you find me?'

'Guy rang Rod's apartment and Rita told him. She and Ben weren't involved, though. Sophie, I'm sorry. Will they let me see Guy?'

'I'm sure they will,' Sophie said softly, and Pru closed her eyes, and then they reached the hospital and Sophie was pushed unceremoniously out of the way as Pru was wheeled inside.

* * * *

Two weeks later just as dusk was falling Sophie and Luke returned to Crispins. Through habit they went into the kitchen and sat by the table. Sophie's hair was once more sleek and black, and Luke's scars no longer troubled him. Sophie wore a new black suit, plain and simple, fitting her perfectly and the short skirt emphasising her long, shapely legs. Luke was dressed in a dark suit and tie. They'd just driven from Heathrow, having attended Gerard's funeral in Bonn the previous day, and coming via Reading where Pru's mother had insisted her daughter be buried.

'Thank you for staying with me,' Sophie said, catching her breath. 'I couldn't have

313

coped on my own, even with Karen and Franz here.'

'I know, funerals are harrowing. Especially two in two days.'

'Poor Pru. I must have been so insensitive not to have realised how much she resented me. On the way to the hospital she didn't stop talking. It all poured out. She said she hadn't meant to do more than threaten me, and I believed her.'

'Yet it sounded as though she helped her husband on his way.'

'How can we tell? He had heart problems, it seemed. No one ever suspected her at the time.'

'She was part of it, from what Ricky's said,' Luke pointed out. 'He's been singing louder than a raven, trying to get out of it. I gather he has more than a few criminal friends, which is where he got the guns.'

'Pru was besotted with Guy, and he took over,' Sophie said sadly.

'She was greedy and ruthless. She could have stopped it when they tried to kill you, but she didn't.'

Sophie nodded. 'There was a message on the machine from Detective Sergeant Pickford. They think they've found Tricia. They want me to go in and identify her.'

'Tricia? The vanishing groom?'

'Yes. Apparently she's Guy's wife. Poor Pru, deceived in that as well!'

'What else did Tricia do, apart from coming here?'

'She once began to train as a nurse, and she was with Guy when they visited Gerard, she had the syringe and injected the air into his vein. She could have got the drugs they used on us, too, from a friend. Apparently she confessed too, when Ricky began to tell all. Ricky, by the way, was the other mysterious visitor who said he was Gerard's brother. He'd gone to spy out the land for them.'

'It's perhaps as well Pru died if she loved him so much. She won't have to see him tried and put in prison for life.'

'Yes.' Sophie fiddled with her handbag on the table in front of her. 'Well, you ought to be off. You'll be in London in an hour now the traffic's quieter. Thanks again for all you've done.'

'Will you sell up here?'

Sophie shook her head vehemently. 'Of course not. I'll find someone to help. There are always girls looking for jobs with horses. I'll manage.'

'Unless you take on a new partner.'

'I don't ever want the complications of a partner again,' she insisted, and looked up to find Luke laughing at her.

'I wouldn't be much help in the stables, apart from occasional mucking out,' he said softly, 'but if you can believe I want you and couldn't care less about your money it's a different sort of partnership I have in mind.'

Sophie looked up at him and her heart began to race. He'd been so distant the past two weeks, since that day they'd come home. He'd been carefully supportive, ready to help in whatever way he could, but had made no sign that he wanted to take up their relationship from where it had reached down in Cornwall. She thought her distrust of him then had stifled the tender feelings he had shown before. Occasionally she'd decided he was remaining just because he had been personally involved and threatened, it was a piece of unfinished business.

'Well?' he asked. 'Am I to go away, or can we start again? You know, when you descended out of that tree I thought my dreams had come true. I didn't know they were going to turn into a nightmare.'

Sophie laughed and moved towards him.

'Luke? Do you mean it? You don't hold it against me for all the horrible things that have happened to you?' She slid her hands beneath his jacket and traced the lines of the scars on his back through his thin shirt.

He pulled her to him and she raised her face for his kiss. When, several minutes later, he released her she was breathless, flushed and dishevelled. 'I've been wanting to do that ever since that first night,' he said, breathless himself.

'Why didn't you?' she asked, provocatively.

'And have you slap my face and accuse me of wanting your money?' he demanded, grinning. 'Sophie, I don't care a damn about your money, I have enough to live on, I might even be able to keep a wife if I'm terribly careful! I suggest you buy up some more land round here and use the money to fund a home for your pensioned horses. Take donkeys too, and mules—they'll remind us not to be silly. But there's one thing I insist on, and that's to promise you'll stop asking me if I mean things!'

She chuckled, and he pulled her to him again. 'If you'd trusted me from the start we might not have got into that mess,' he whispered.

'And we might not have caught them.'

'I see, opinionated as well as bossy. What kind of a wife am I getting?'

'I don't know. You haven't asked anyone to marry you yet.'

He eyed her in amusement. 'I've been restraining myself for months, ever since we met.'

Suddenly she laughed. 'Do you have to go back to your flat tonight? For pity's sake take off that jacket and tie, I'm not used to seeing you dressed so formally. And I want to check, very carefully, on how your scars are progressing. Maybe, when there's a lull, you'll get around to asking me.'

'Maybe I will,' he replied, and she went back into his arms with a sigh of pleasure. It felt so right with his arms around her, his lips on hers, and his hands caressing her and promising untold delights to come.

'I think I'd like a bath,' she murmured into his shoulder. 'And there's a bottle of champagne somewhere.'

'You mean you want to be really decadent with bubbles in the bath and in the champagne glasses?' he demanded.

'My stomach feels all bubbly,' she said,

laughing up at him.

'That isn't your stomach, wench! Don't be so unromantic. That's your heart.'

Smiling, arms entwined, they carried the champagne and the glasses upstairs. Sophie thought that, despite the losses of the last few weeks, and the perils they'd faced together, she'd never before been so happy. An hour later, as they sat up in the crumpled bed and Luke opened the bottle, she knew that she'd merely sipped at the many and wonderful delights that lay waiting for her in her new life.

This Large Print Book for the Partially sighted, who cannot read normal print, is published under the auspices of

THE ULVERSCROFT FOUNDATION